"Are you...the one?"

"Uh...the one?" Ben asked.

"The one who's going to finally get me pregnant?"

Ben completely lost his train of thought. He stared at her.

Natalie leaned against the door and winced. "I just woke up. But I feel so..." She seemed to sink, about to fall.

He reached for her and pushed her gently back toward the bed. Her hands clasped his arms and held on.

Natalie's eyes looked into his, their gray depths almost lucid. He felt her tension in the grip of her fingers.

"You are him," she whispered.

She looked so grave. What was she talking about? "Who?" Ben asked.

"The father of my baby," she replied.

Dear Reader,

Heartwarming, emotional, compelling...these are all words that describe Harlequin American Romance. Check out this month's stellar selection of love stories, which are sure to delight you.

First, Debbi Rawlins delivers the exciting conclusion of Harlequin American Romance's continuity series, TEXAS SHEIKHS. In *His Royal Prize*, sparks fly immediately between dashing sheikh Sharif and Desert Rose ranch hand Olivia Smith. However, Sharif never expected their romantic tryst to be plastered all over the tabloids—or that the only way to salvage their reputations would be to make Olivia his royal bride.

Bestselling author Muriel Jensen pens another spectacular story in her WHO'S THE DADDY? miniseries with *Daddy To Be Determined*, in which a single gal's ticking biological clock leads her to convince a single dad that he's the perfect man to father her baby. In *Have Husband, Need Honeymoon*, the third book in Rita Herron's THE HARTWELL HOPE CHESTS miniseries, Alison Hartwell thought her youthful marriage to an air force pilot had been annulled, but surprise! Now a forced reunion with her "husband" has her wondering if a second honeymoon couldn't give them a second chance at forever. And Harlequin American Romance's promotion THE WAY WE MET...AND MARRIED continues with *The Best Blind Date in Texas*. Don't miss this wonderful romance from Victoria Chancellor.

It's a great lineup, and we hope you enjoy them all!

Wishing you happy reading,

Melissa Jeglinski
Associate Senior Editor
Harlequin American Romance

MURIEL JENSEN
Daddy To Be
Determined

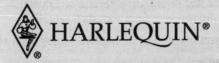
HARLEQUIN®

TORONTO • NEW YORK • LONDON
AMSTERDAM • PARIS • SYDNEY • HAMBURG
STOCKHOLM • ATHENS • TOKYO • MILAN • MADRID
PRAGUE • WARSAW • BUDAPEST • AUCKLAND

To Austin and Jordan Jensen, with love from Grandma.

ISBN 0-373-16882-9

DADDY TO BE DETERMINED

Copyright © 2001 by Muriel Jensen.

Visit us at www.eHarlequin.com

Printed in U.S.A.

ABOUT THE AUTHOR

Muriel Jensen and her husband, Ron, live in Astoria, Oregon, in an old foursquare Victorian at the mouth of the Columbia River. They share their home with a golden retriever/golden Labrador mix named Amber, and five cats who moved in with them without an invitation. (Muriel insists that a plate of Friskies and a bowl of water are *not* an invitation!)

They also have three children and their families in their lives—a veritable crowd of the most interesting people and children. They also have irreplaceable friends, wonderful neighbors and "a life they know they don't deserve but love desperately anyway."

Books by Muriel Jensen

HARLEQUIN AMERICAN ROMANCE

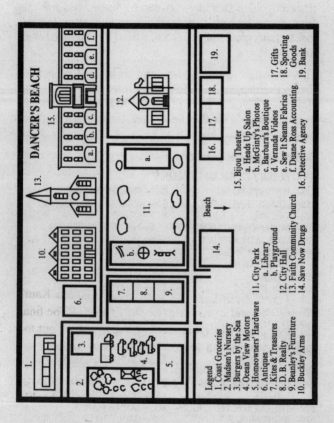

DANCER'S BEACH

Legend
1. Coast Groceries
2. Madsen's Nursery
3. Burgers by the Sea
4. Ocean View Motors
5. Homeowners' Hardware
6. Antiques
7. Kites & Treasures
8. D. B. Realty
9. Beanley's Furniture
10. Buckley Arms

11. City Park
   a. Library
   b. Playground
12. City Hall
13. Faith Community Church
14. Save Now Drugs

15. Bijou Theater
   a. Heads Up Salon
   b. McGinty's Photos
   c. Barbara's Boutique
   d. Veranda Videos
   e. Sew It Seams Fabrics
   f. Duane Ross Accounting
16. Detective Agency
17. Gifts
18. Sporting Goods
19. Bank

Beach →

Prologue

Natalie Browning sat in the middle of her darkened living room and watched the nightly news, a pillow pulled up to her face just below her eyes. Delia Jones, her former assistant at KRTV and now a weekend anchor for KXAV, had called twenty minutes ago to warn her about Karen Kaufman's lead story.

The beautiful redhead with the face of a Mucha model and the heart of a viper smiled benevolently at the camera.

"Welcome to Channel 4 News. I'm Karen Kaufman," she said in a flawlessly clear voice. "The final chapter of the Moss Laboratories story played out to-day in court when Donald Parker was indicted on seventeen counts of fraud, thanks to the tireless efforts of Philadelphia's KRTV newswoman, Natalie Browning, who was herself a victim of the sperm bank's deceptions.

"Her investigation uncovered Parker's practice of creating false donor profiles and filling orders with his own sperm. The ruse was uncovered when Browning's fertility specialist requested a second delivery of sperm from the laboratory, after the first attempt at impregnation proved unsuccessful."

Natty felt pain and humiliation splash over her like a cold shower. She clutched the pillow more tightly.

"When that also failed," Karen continued with what appeared to be genuine concern, "Browning's doctor had the sperm sample analyzed, thinking he might discover that it hadn't been handled properly in the transfer from the laboratory. What he discovered instead was that the sperm was indeed motile, but that both samples had precisely the same DNA pattern—and therefore the same donor."

"And that the impregnation problem," Natalie said to the television, her voice thick because she had a head cold, "lies with Browning and not with the sperm. Thank you, Karen. Kind of you to point that out."

"Investigation of other samples proved that Parker had been perpetrating his scam for some time," the redhead continued relentlessly. "The laboratory has been closed pending the outcome of the trial."

She could have lived through that, Natty thought, pressing a tissue to her sniffly nose, but the last segment was a feature called "Celebrity Dish"—a sort of gossip roundup dispensed by Jolie Ramirez, a perky brunette who loved uncovering the most embarrassing details about the most notable people.

Tonight it seemed that a male vocalist was in rehab, an actress on Broadway beat her baseball-playing husband's Jaguar with his own bat, and "Natalie Browning, the darling of the nightly news on Philadelphia's Channel 6, apparently is no one's darling at home, considering her story about Moss Laboratories, the now-infamous sperm bank. It was a story she stumbled upon while availing herself of the lab's services.

"'She appears beautiful and sexy,'" according to an old boyfriend who preferred to remain anonymous, "'but she has the cold heart of an old maid. No wonder she had to go to a sperm bank.'"

Natalie stared at the screen, aghast, then threw her pillow at it, barely suppressing a scream. That action brought on a coughing fit.

She knew the anonymous former boyfriend was Artie Webb, producer of the Channel 4 nightly news, whose advances she'd spurned at a weekend news conference in Boston three years earlier. He'd been married at the time—to Karen Kaufman—but his ego had never forgiven Natalie. Jolie Ramirez, unfortunately, was just doing her job.

Natalie clicked off the television, called the airport and made a reservation to fly out to Portland, Oregon, on the red-eye. Then she went into her bedroom to pack.

Tomorrow morning she'd probably be front page news and the subject of every radio talk show on the Atlantic seaboard. She didn't want to be around for that, and she still had four weeks left of the three-month leave she'd taken to get pregnant.

Six weeks ago, the story had developed and the professional in her had come to the fore, pushing her own concerns aside in the interest of protecting and informing the public.

She'd suspected as she had filed the story that she

might become part of the news—an undesirable consequence for any good reporter. But she hadn't counted on Channel 4 taking its exploration of her involvement in the story to such lengths.

Even as she threw clothes haphazardly into her suitcase, she understood that such things happened. Enemies in the business were vengeful, and the only response was silence.

But this was the final straw in a long series of events that conspired to make her feel like a failure as a woman. What, after all, could contribute to that feeling more completely than the inability to reproduce, and having that news spread over the entire East Coast network?

She threw several pairs of shoes into her case, along with her makeup bag, an extra box of tissues and several chunky sweaters. Dancer's Beach, Oregon, would be chilly in November.

She was willing to admit to herself that she was running away, and she knew that was probably cowardly. But she needed a comforting shoulder and there was nobody around who could provide one.

Her mother had been against the whole sperm bank thing in the beginning and was happy to say "I told you so." Natalie's brothers were geniuses, but generally clueless about her. And what friends she had time for in her busy schedule all had husbands and children, and she couldn't burden them with her problems.

But she'd recently reconnected with her cousin Dori in Dancer's Beach. They'd been great friends as children, and Natty suddenly longed for her smiling understanding.

It occurred to her seven hours later, at about nine o'clock the following morning, that it would have been wise to call first, despite the lateness of the hour when she'd made her decision. Because there was no one home.

A smiling older man walking by with a golden retriever on a leash said politely, "The Dominguez family is away for a few weeks." His eyes went to her suitcase, then to her probably puffy face and red nose. "Is it important that you reach them?"

She sighed and shook her head. The long plane ride had made it feel like a brick with ears. "No, thank you." She walked down the steps and was snuffled by the friendly dog. "I made a last minute decision to visit without calling first. Can you recommend a motel?"

The man pointed up the street. "See that green-and-white Craftsman on the corner? That's Lulu Griffin's B-and-B. Very comfortable. Good food. And Nugget and I just walked by. The Vacancy sign is out."

"Thank you." Natalie shook his hand. "I appreciate your help."

"It was my pleasure."

As the man and the dog walked on, Natalie headed for the bed-and-breakfast, barely able to breathe, and feeling lower than she'd ever felt in all her twenty-six years. With her demanding mother and her genius brothers, she'd always felt inadequate.

Then, after years of trying to fit a little social life

into her busy schedule and finding the singles scene soul-deadening, she'd met Kyle Wagner. A young actor with fire and passion, he'd seemed like her dream come true. Until they'd become engaged and his fire and passion turned to complacency and only mild interest in her life.

But she'd wanted a baby more than she wanted anything, and she'd almost settled for Kyle—until he told her he didn't want children until he was in his forties.

She'd broken the engagement and turned to the sperm bank. And then she hadn't been able to become pregnant, even under perfect conditions.

What was left for her? she wondered as she climbed the steps of the B-and-B. She now had no man, no baby and very probably no job.

Nothing could save her now. Natalie Felicia Browning had blown her life.

Chapter One

Ben Griffin lifted five-year-old Roxanne out of the bathtub and wrapped her in a thick blue towel. He sat on the closed lid of the john with her and helped her dry off. She had his dark eyes and hair, though hers hung in thick ringlets—when it wasn't snarled in knots.

"I wanted to wash my hair," she complained as she held tightly to Betsy, a small rag doll with black button eyes and a painted heart-shaped mouth. "Julie Callahan Griffin made that," he used to remind himself when the pain of her loss had been so enormous he had to say her name or burst. The doll was never more than a hand's span away from Roxie, awake or sleeping.

"We washed your hair yesterday," Ben reminded her.

"Vannie gets to wash her hair every day," she argued.

"Vannie has very short hair. And she blows it dry." Vanessa was seven, and the decision to cut her hair had come at the end of the summer, when she'd returned from camp. She hadn't explained why she wanted to cut her long, golden-brown hair, but she'd been adamant.

Since their mother had died a year and a half ago, Ben had done his best to allow them whatever was in his power and wouldn't hurt them.

Roxie swung her head from side to side so that her long hair flew out. It would have slapped him in the face if he hadn't drawn back.

She giggled, then declared, "I don't want to cut my hair."

"I don't blame you," he said, helping her into lavender flannel pajamas patterned with pink kittens and blue puppies. "It's very pretty."

"Can I wear lipstick to Marianne's tomorrow?"

Marianne Beasley owned and operated the day care where Roxie spent several hours every day.

"Nope," Ben replied. She asked this question every night. "Sorry."

"Can I get my ears pierced?"

This was a new question. Having finished putting her pajamas on, he turned her toward him to look into her eyes. They were bright and frighteningly intelligent. "Do you even know what that is?"

"Yeah," she said, pulling her little lobe out for him to see. "A lady sticks it with a needle and it doesn't even hurt! She puts a little hole right there and you can wear different earrings in them every day."

"No," he said, knowing he had to say it firmly or she'd be cajoling him all night long. "You have to wait until you grow up a little more."

She looked indignant. "I'm five! Paloma has pierced ears, and she's only four!"

"I'm sorry. That's the way it is."

"Can I have ice cream before bed?"

He lifted her onto his hip and carried her downstairs, wondering if part of her strategy was to ask for the impossible, knowing she could bargain him down. Ice cream at night sometimes gave her a stomachache, but tonight he'd risk it in the interest of making her feel less deprived.

The telephone rang when he was halfway down the stairs.

"I'll get it!" Vanessa shouted.

When he rounded the corner into the kitchen, he saw that she was already dressed for bed. She used his bathroom at night and always got herself ready without fuss. He wondered if she was the only second-grader in the world with a tidy sock drawer and clothes on hangers instead of all over her room.

He worried a little about her efficiency at such a tender age but reminded himself that Julie had been a stickler for tidiness and order. Vanessa came by it naturally.

"He's right here, Grandma." Vanessa put her hand over the mouthpiece and handed the telephone to him. "Grandma's having trouble with a guest," she whispered.

"Thank you." He put Roxie on her feet. "Van, can you scoop up some ice cream for you and Roxie?"

She looked surprised. "At night?"

"Just tonight."

"How come?"

"Because I said so."

With a shrug, Vanessa pulled open the door of the side-by-side refrigerator and delved into the freezer at the bottom.

"Ha!" his mother said into his ear. "You used to get upset when I gave you that answer, and now *you're* doing it. The best revenge is watching you become me."

"Thanks to the gender difference," he said, backing onto a stool near the counter, "that'll only go so far. What's up?"

"Well…" She made a small sound of distress. "I'm not entirely sure. Do you know Natalie Browning?"

"No," he replied. He'd never been wild about his mother buying a seven-bedroom house and turning it into a bed-and-breakfast, inviting complete strangers to be locked in with her at night without benefit of any information about them except their names. "Why?"

"I think she's a celebrity in the East. Her driver's license says Philadelphia. When I asked her what brought her to Dancer's Beach, she said something about needing to hide out from cameras and publicity."

"Interesting." He watched Vanessa struggle with the ice cream scoop, and was about to get up and help her when she went to the sink and ran it under the hot water. She tried again and the ice cream scooped out easily. He wondered if Julie had taught her that. What a kid. "Never heard of her."

"Well, she arrived yesterday looking as though her only friend had died. And I haven't seen her since, except peeking out from behind her door. Today I haven't seen her at all.''

''Have you knocked? Or called?''

''She doesn't answer.''

''Maybe she's just sleeping.''

His mother sighed. ''I think it's worse than that. She had a terrible cold, so I mixed her a hot toddy with my apricot brandy. I left her the bottle, and I haven't seen her or it since.''

''Sounds as though you have a guest on a bender, Mom. What do you want me to do?''

''I told her she could have that room for only one night. It's reserved for a pair of honeymooners who are due in less than two hours. Would you...come and talk to her? Beautiful women always respond to handsome men.''

''Mom...'' He groaned. She was always finding some excuse to introduce him to some young woman or get him invited to some event where single women would be present. Between her and Marianne Beasley, who came on to him at every opportunity, he was clutching his bachelorhood with both hands.

''It has nothing to do with that!'' she said firmly. She'd always read his mind. He hated that she could still do it. ''I'm simply trying to take care of a difficult matter in a discreet and civilized way. I don't want to call the police or make a fuss, because she looks like a woman who's had enough trouble, but if you're too busy for me...''

''The girls are just out of the bath,'' he pleaded, ''and eating their snacks before bed.''

''I said that was fine,'' she repeated stiffly. He

could imagine her, wounded look in place on her carefully made up face, spiked white hair even spikier in her imagined state of neglect. "If you're too busy, I'll just—"

"We'll be there." He caved; it was inevitable. "Give me ten minutes."

"You can have twelve," she said. "Thank you, Ben."

"Sure." He hung up the phone. "Get your slippers and coats," he said to the girls. "Put away the ice cream. We're going to Grandma's."

They hurried to comply, and he had to smile as he watched them run upstairs. Coming home to Dancer's Beach to give them a sense of family after Julie died had been a good idea. They loved their grandmother, who didn't seem to persecute them the way she picked on him, and their Sunday evening dinners at the B-and-B were enjoyed by all of them.

He just hoped he survived the move. Leaving his work in Portland as a developer of high-density urban dwellings and purchasing the Bijou Theater Building in downtown Dancer's Beach left him more time to be with the girls. However, their standard of living had taken a considerable dive, though he seemed to be the only one who noticed.

The old lodge-style house on a hill overlooking the town had been in serious need of repair. But, licensed in plumbing and wiring, he'd made short shrift of the major problems and was working slowly on giving the place a facelift.

He kept thinking he'd adjusted to life without Julie. Then Vanessa, who looked so much like her, would smile at him with an arched eyebrow, or Roxie would fold her arms in displeasure, and he was ambushed by old memories and ever-present longings.

He'd bought the house to keep him busy. Evenings after the girls had gone to bed were difficult, but Sundays were abominable. They'd always done special things on Sunday—picnics, sight-seeing, driving to the coast. With Saturday's chores done and Monday's responsibilities not yet upon them, they were particularly carefree.

Though the pace of his life had slowed considerably, Ben felt as though he never had a carefree moment anymore. He worried about the girls constantly, hoping he was giving them everything they needed, knowing it was impossible for a father to do so.

Slippers and coats on, Betsy tucked into Roxie's pocket, the girls raced past him and out the door to the indigo van emblazoned with his logo and company name, Bijou Development.

He smiled as he followed in their wake. At least he didn't have to worry about their physical well-being. He wished he could move that energetically.

LOUISE GRIFFIN'S bed-and-breakfast could only be described, Ben thought, as "country coordinates gone mad." The living room, which flowed into the dining room, was wallpapered from ceiling to waist height in an all-over rose-and-ivy pattern that had a coordinating border of tightly clustered roses. Then a rose-and-green-striped paper swept down to the rose-colored baseboards.

Every room in the house was similarly decorated,

though the motifs and colors were different. Every bedroom had coordinating papers and border, as well as bedding and curtains that also matched. Each bed had several sets of pillows, all mix and match, like something out of a linens ad.

Looking at them too long made him crazy, as though there was no room for free thought, and everything in the world had to coordinate with or match everything else.

But his mother loved it and apparently so did her guests. Ben did her books, and after only three years, she was doing very well.

The girls rushed into the kitchen, where his mother had a small table and a television. She stood at the counter, placing cookies on a plate, and they stopped briefly to greet her.

She leaned down to sweep them into her arms. Then she handed Roxie the plate and Vanessa two glasses of milk.

"You two eat up while your dad and I do business."

"With the drunk guest?" Vanessa asked as Roxie ran over to the television.

"We don't know that she's drunk," his mother admonished gently. "I'm just worried about her. Go on, now."

Vanessa followed Roxie.

Ben waited for his mother in the kitchen doorway. She didn't look like anybody's mother. She was medium height and slender in velvety lavender top and slacks as coordinated as her rooms. A pendant with a large purple-and-green stone hung around her neck.

She had short white hair that was moussed and spiked, and she wore more makeup than he thought she needed, but that wasn't his call.

She liked to in-line skate in her free time, and was known occasionally to add gin to her Citrucel.

She'd never been a cuddly mother, but she'd always adored him, and what he'd lacked in hugs and snuggles, she'd made up for by being there for him every time he turned to her for help. When Julie died, Lulu had left a friend in charge of the B-and-B and come to stay with him for a month to help the girls and do all the paperwork chores, such as death certificates and insurance notifications, that he simply hadn't had the heart for.

She'd cooked, too, though even Roxie had noticed that they ate a lot of egg dishes and fancy pancakes.

"Well, she has a bed-and-*breakfast*," Vanessa had pointed out with surprising insight. "Breakfast is all she gets to cook."

Lulu did seem worried as she hooked her arm in his now and led him into the dining room. Several guests occupied the living room and were in cheerful conversation about their respective vacations.

"I want to do this with a minimum of fuss," she said quietly, smiling as one of the guests waved at her. "Miss Browning didn't come down to breakfast and she was really under the weather yesterday."

Ben nodded. "I understand that, Mom. I just don't know why you think I'm the one to handle this."

"Because you're my troubleshooter. You fix everything around here."

"But this is a person. Not a pipe or an electrical connection."

"You were very good with Julie, and she was a complex, sometimes volatile woman."

"I was married to Julie."

"You're good with everyone." Lulu physically turned him toward the hallway and the stairs. "Just please make sure she's okay, then explain that she has to leave. She's in the Woodsy Cabin Room on the third floor. All the other guests on that floor are out. Her name's Natalie!" she whispered after him.

Right. The Woodsy Cabin Room was the one with pine tree motif paper at the top, brown bears gamboling over the paper on the bottom, and the whole of it brought together by green border paper patterned with moose.

He had to be insane, Ben thought as he climbed two flights of stairs, to let his mom bully him into this. What did a man say to a strange woman clearly on a lost weekend?

He drew a breath, prayed that he would create as small a scene as possible, and knocked on the door.

He was surprised when it opened immediately. And he was quite literally rendered speechless by the woman who stood there. She wore only a red-and-black flannel shirt and red-toed boot socks. She was fairly tall, five-foot-nine or -ten, and her legs from the tail of her shirt to her ankles were something to behold—shapely, milky white and very, very long.

He dragged his eyes away abruptly, concentrating on his mission. But gazing into her face wasn't easy on him, either. She had wide gray eyes that appeared a little vague, but were filled with an expression that mingled pain and sadness—two things with which he was very familiar. Her nose was small and came to a delicate—if red—point, her lips were nicely shaped but pale, her chin was gently rounded and her face was a perfect oval.

A short, unruly mop of golden-blond hair stood up in disarray. She peered at him with unfocused eyes. In the hand that held the door open was a small, flat box.

She looked like a cross between Michelle Pfeiffer and Jenna Elfman. Ben found himself touched by the look in her eyes. He couldn't even think about her legs.

He forced himself to remember why he was here, and opened his mouth to speak.

But she asked abruptly, "Are you...the one?" She weaved a little as she peered at him more closely.

"Uh...the one?"

"The one," she repeated, making a wide gesture with the box. It was apparently empty. "The one who's going to finally get me pregnant."

He completely lost his train of thought. He stared at her.

"'Cause Dori told me..." She leaned against the door and winced, rubbing her head. "But I thought it was a dream." She spoke slowly, her voice slurred. "I just woke up. But I feel so..." She dropped the box and seemed to sink, about to fall.

He reached for the box instinctively and caught it, then grabbed for her and pushed her gently back toward the bed. Her hands clasped his arms and held on.

Her eyes looked into his, their gray depths almost lucid. He felt her tension in the grip of her fingers.

"You *are* him," she whispered.

She looked so grave. What *was* she talking about? "Who?" he asked, lowering his voice unconsciously.

"The father of my baby," she replied.

"I'm...Lulu's son," he said, pulling the edge of the coverlet over her knees.

"Lulu?"

"She owns this place."

The woman looked around the room. "The... clinic?"

"No, this isn't a clinic. You're staying at a bed-and-breakfast."

She frowned, apparently trying to absorb that. "Why?"

"I don't know," he replied. "You've been sick." He held up the box and saw that it contained extra-strength cold medication. "I think you've had a cold." He tossed the box at the bedside table and noted the empty toddy mug there. The brandy bottle stood beside it.

She fell back onto the mattress, then put a finger to her lips. "Sick. But...shh! Or they'll report that I'm dying!"

He didn't even try to understand what that meant. He reached for the bottle and held it up to the light. It was still mostly full, though he guessed even a small amount of brandy with strong cold medication could reduce someone to such a state.

"How many pills have you had?" he asked.

She put a hand to her head. "Um...five...eight. Not sure."

"You should eat something," he suggested. "Maybe drink some coffee." He pulled the coverlet all the way over her. "I'll go get—"

She caught his shirtsleeve with surprising strength, preventing him from straightening up. "I just want the baby," she said. "Now. Before I..."

He guessed she'd been about to say, "Before I pass out," because then she did just that.

"Oh boy," Ben grumbled to himself as he placed a pillow under her head. She was crackers, but he probably was, too. After a year and a half of celibacy, making a baby with a gorgeous blonde didn't sound half-bad.

But he preferred his women conscious.

His women, he thought with dry amusement. As though he'd had any. It had been him and Julie since high school. He'd never had another lover. And he didn't want another one now. He fully intended to live out his life in quiet frustration, because there couldn't be another woman with whom he fit so perfectly in every way. Like the damned wallpaper.

"Oh, my God," his mother said, coming to lean beside him as he tried to assess the woman's condition. "What did you do?"

He turned to her impatiently. "I didn't do anything. She passed out, thanks to your heavy-handed toddy and a box of cold pills."

"Did you tell her she has to be out tonight?"

"I didn't get a chance to tell her much of anything.

She mistook me for someone who's supposed to get her pregnant.''

"What?"

"I don't know. At one point she thought she was dreaming. What are you doing?"

His mother was walking around the room, putting the few things left out into the open suitcase on the luggage rack.

"I've got to move her so I can prepare this room," she said. She took a cosmetics bag off the dresser and tossed it in.

"Where are you going to put her?"

His mother gasped in reply, her eyes widening as she stared at a newspaper she'd picked up with the cosmetics bag.

He went to read over her shoulder.

News Anchor Scammed by Casanova of Sperm Lab. The headline was two inches high, in bold print. The subhead read, Newswoman Courageously Turns Table on Sperm Lab Doctor Filling Orders with his Own Sperm.

"Poor thing!" his mother exclaimed as Ben scanned the story. "She goes to a sperm lab for help getting pregnant and learns that she's been defrauded. But she had the courage to play out the story and bring the man to trial. Fortunately for her, the procedure didn't work."

It was a sad story. He suddenly understood her insistence about getting pregnant.

"And knowing that," Ben said, "you can throw her out in the cold?"

"No," Lulu said, dropping the paper into a pretty trash basket. "I can let you take her home with you."

Ben glared at her. "Mom…"

"What else am I going to do? I have guests arriving in less than two hours."

"You can find her a room at another—"

"The Buckley Arms is full—the crafters convention. And I'm it for B-and-Bs."

He struggled to hold on to his good humor. "I'm *not* a B-and-B, Mom. I'm a working man with two little—"

"I know, I know," she said, patting his cheek. "But she's clearly in a state that requires she be looked after, and I can't do that with an inn filled with guests. You, on the other hand, always manage to look after everyone in your life very well."

"But she's not in my life," he insisted, "she's in yours."

"But I'm in yours, sweetie. See? It's logical. Scientific, even. Mathematical, sort of. She's in mine and I'm in yours, therefore she's in yours, too."

"God."

Chapter Two

Vanessa and Roxie skipped after him as he carried a still-sleeping Natalie Browning, wrapped in a blanket, out to the van. His mother followed with the suitcase.

"She's so pretty!" Vanessa exclaimed as he placed Natalie on the front passenger seat, tilting it back to help keep her in place.

"Like Sleeping Beauty!" Roxie said.

His mother slid the side door open and put the suitcase into the back seat.

Vanessa tucked Natalie's feet in.

"If you kiss her, Daddy, she'll wake up!" Roxie added.

His mother smiled at him and said under her breath, "And maybe you will, too, Ben."

He sent her a dark look. "You're already on dangerous ground, Mom. She can stay on the sofa tonight, but first thing in the morning she's on her own."

"Of course." She reached up to kiss his cheek as he closed the door on his unexpected houseguest. Lulu blew kisses to the girls and hurried back inside.

Roxie stood between the two front seats when he

climbed in behind the wheel. She looked down at the young woman, patting the disheveled blond hair with a pudgy little hand.

"I wish my hair was this color," she said.

Vanessa, leaning over the back of the front seat, handed the seat belt to Roxie, who clicked it into place.

"Yeah, me too," Vanessa replied. "I'd wear it long with lots of curls."

"Can we keep her, Daddy?" Roxie asked promptly.

"She's not a puppy, Rox," he said patiently. "When she wakes up, I'm sure she's going to want to go home."

Actually, she might not, he thought as he backed the van out onto the street. Judging by the newspaper article, things must have been difficult for her there. The article had included a rude comment from an old boyfriend of hers and his suggestion that she wasn't the beautiful, sweet woman she appeared to be on television.

"Can we keep her till she wakes up?"

"She'll be awake in the morning," Ben assured his daughter.

"If you don't kiss her, she won't."

"She's *not* Sleeping Beauty," Vanessa told Roxie. "She's just a lady that's asleep. Grandma said she's on television."

"Right." Ben took the turn that would lead them home. "She does the news at night. Like Peter Jennings."

In the rearview mirror he saw Roxie wrinkle her nose. "The news!"

"It's an important job," Vanessa informed her. "Daddy watches it all the time. That's how you learn what's going on in other places."

To Roxie, who cared mostly about her room, her house and Marianne's Day Care, that seemed irrelevant.

"She can sleep in the other twin bed in my room, Daddy," Vanessa offered. "So she isn't afraid when she wakes up."

He'd told his mother that he intended to put Natalie on the sofa, but he'd just repainted the fourth bedroom upstairs and put the futon from the family room in it. She'd be comfortable there, and he'd be more likely to hear her if she woke up in the middle of the night, wondering what had happened and where she was.

He turned into their driveway, which was lit by floodlights at the front of the house. He hit the garage door opener and pulled into the dimly lit interior.

The girls scrambled out and went ahead of him to open doors.

He scooped Natalie Browning out of the front seat and into his arms. She lay limply against him, the scent of gardenias intermingled with the smell of a mentholated rub.

He remembered her looking into his eyes and telling him that he was "the one." The one her dream had sent to give her a baby.

He walked into the house with her, as Vanessa held the kitchen door open. He couldn't help wondering why a beautiful young woman would have gone to a sperm bank in the first place. Unless the boyfriend quoted in the article was right and she *was* cold and forbidding.

It was hard to tell when he'd spoken to her only while she'd been incoherent. But she didn't look like a cold-hearted woman.

Roxie held open the door to the fourth bedroom upstairs. Vanessa, running along behind him, asked him to wait while she got a sheet and blankets out of the linen closet.

She and Roxie spread a flannel sheet over the plain red futon.

"I'll get one of my pillows," Vanessa said, and ran off.

"She should have something to sleep with," Roxie said. She took Betsy out of her pocket, studied the doll with a worried frown, then placed it beside Natalie. But before she could even remove her hands from it, she reconsidered and pressed Betsy to her chest.

"I'll get Starla for her!" Roxie said, clearly pleased to have come up with a solution that did not involve parting with Betsy. Starla was a large stuffed bear who'd lost his right button eye. Julie had covered the large hole with a star-shaped piece of yellow felt stitched into place. Roxie loved the bear's new personality and had even renamed it appropriately.

When Ben had suggested that the name was feminine and not masculine, Vanessa had taken her sister's side. "Only girls have stars in their eyes, Daddy, so she must be a girl."

Well, he'd learned something new.

He lay Natalie down on the flannel sheet and the blanket she'd been wrapped in. Vanessa arrived just in time to put a pillow under her head. Roxie put Starla beside Natalie and made sure that Ben covered her, too, when he opened out the top sheet, then a pink thermal blanket and spread them over the bed. Not certain one blanket would keep her warm enough, he sent Vanessa to the linen closet for another.

Natalie stirred restlessly as Ben spread the second blanket. Her brow furrowed and she moaned as though something hurt.

"What's the matter with her?" Vanessa asked worriedly.

Instinctively, Ben put a hand to Natalie's cheek. "Probably just a bad dream," he guessed. He noticed with a start that her skin was like satin to the touch.

She smiled, just a very small curve of her lips. Then she reached out, as though groping for something, her fingers spread wide.

Again, instinctively, he caught them in his. Her hand tightened around his with a strength that demonstrated how desperate she'd been for that contact. At least in her sleep. Loneliness, he knew, was a powerful enemy.

"She likes you, Daddy!" Roxie whispered loudly.

Vanessa looked at him a little worriedly, and he was just wondering himself if he was going to have to lean over this bed for the rest of the night when Natalie made a contented little sound, freed his hand and rolled onto her side.

He felt enormous relief as he readjusted her blankets.

He ushered the girls out into the hallway and pulled the door halfway closed.

"Can we have our ice cream now?" Roxie asked.

"We had ice cream at Grandma's," Vanessa ratted, to Roxie's chagrin. "And cookies, too."

"Then I think we're finished for tonight." Ben picked up Roxie under one arm and Vanessa under the other, to their squealing delight. He had to keep reminding himself to play with them more often, to remember that they needed him to be cheerful and hopeful.

He tended to get bogged down in work and memories and forget that a child learned a lot by having fun.

He dropped Roxie onto her bed and, with Vanessa still tucked under his arm, leaned over her to kiss her good-night. The girls collided and giggled hysterically.

He carried Vanessa out with him across the hall to her room and dropped her in her bed.

"Can she stay for dinner tomorrow?" she asked, sitting up in bed.

"Roxie?" he asked, fluffing the one pillow Van had left. "Yes, we have to let her stay for dinner. It's part of the family deal. You have to feed the kids."

"Daddy!" Vanessa slapped his arm. "I mean the lady. Can she stay for dinner? If she isn't awake when I go to school, I won't even hear her talk or anything."

That confused him for a moment. "Hear her talk?"

She hunched a shoulder. "Yeah. You know. I bet she has a pretty voice, 'specially if she's on television. And I miss Mom's voice." She looked at him from under thick dark lashes. "Is it okay to say that?"

He sat down on the edge of her bed, anguished by that question. "Van, it's okay for you to say whatever you're feeling. I asked you to tell me when you miss her and feel lonely."

She nodded quickly. "I know. And I do. But I had just turned six then. Now I've been seven for a while and it doesn't make me cry anymore when I miss her, and I know I have to make believe everything's okay." She gave him a look that told him she understood far more than he realized. "That's what you do, 'cause you're the dad. So, I do it, too, 'cause I'm the big sister. But it would be nice to hear the lady's voice, if we can't ever hear Mom's again."

Her perception always amazed him. He didn't know why he was surprised that she'd understood he pretended cheer and hope when he didn't feel it.

"Sometimes," he said, ruffling her short, shaggy hair, "if you pretend something awful is really okay, it eventually makes it okay. Or at least makes it hurt less." He pinched her chin. "But you don't ever have to pretend what you don't feel, Vannie. You can always tell me what you're thinking, even if you're afraid I won't like it."

"I know." She lay back against her pillows and smiled up at him. "I'm not afraid to tell you anything. I just don't want to make you sad if you're not by talking about me being sad."

He drew her blankets up and leaned down to kiss

her cheek. "But I'd be really sad if you were sad and didn't tell me."

She smiled. "I'm not sad right now. I'm anxious to wake up in the morning and see what the lady's like. Promise if she isn't awake when I go to school, you'll ask her to stay for dinner so I can talk to her."

That didn't sound like a good idea, but he couldn't deny her. "I promise."

"Okay. Good night, Daddy."

"Good night, baby."

"I'm not a baby."

"You'll be *my* baby until you're ninety."

Vanessa smiled tolerantly, appreciating her precious status, though still offended by the name. "Roxie's the baby."

"I am not!" The protest came indignantly from across the hall. "I've five! And I'm gonna get pierced ears!"

Vanessa sat up, competitive edge honed. "She is?" she demanded of Ben. "When?"

Ben shouted across the hall. "When, Roxie?"

There was silence for several seconds, then Roxie replied grudgingly. "When I'm grown up. But I'm gonna get three in each ear!"

Pleased that she hadn't missed a rite of passage, Vanessa fell back on her pillow. "She's such a fibber!" she said.

"I am not!"

"She was just anticipating," Ben said. "You know what that is?"

"It's like thinking about it, only before it happens."

"Very good."

Ben covered her again, kissed her cheek and turned off her bedside lamp. "Good night, woman of great wisdom," he said grandly.

She giggled. "That's better, Daddy."

He kissed her again and went across the hall to where Roxie sat up in bed, her expression pugnacious, her arms folded. "I'm *not* a baby," she declared clearly. "I'm the littlest, but I'm not a baby."

"You're absolutely right," he said, gently pushing her back and pulling up her covers.

"I can pour my own milk if you don't buy the really big bottle with the handle, and I know about looking both ways to cross the street, and I don't cry when I fall down."

"Yes, I know."

"At Marianne's I can swing higher than Austin O'Brian, and he's six!"

She was the most adventurous child at the day care center—Marianne had told him that several times. Ben liked knowing she wasn't afraid but hoped she'd acquire her sister's sense of self-preservation before she did herself any real harm.

"I know you act like a big girl," he praised her, taking her rag doll from the coverlet and putting it in her hands. "But you and Vanessa were such pretty babies that I still think of you that way sometimes."

Roxie was a pushover for flattery. She smiled benevolently. "That's okay, Daddy. What time is the lady going to wake up?"

"I don't know, Rox. We'll let tomorrow take care of itself, okay?"

Her pristine little brow puckered. "What does that mean?"

"It means we won't worry about what happens tomorrow until it's tomorrow."

"Oh. Am I going to Marianne's right after breakfast?"

"Yes. I have to put a new water heater in the building tomorrow and I'd like to get an early start. Is that okay with you?"

"Yeah. We're going to make turkeys tomorrow by drawing our hands. That's going to be fun."

He tried to imagine how that would work and couldn't. "Good." He leaned down to hug her and got a big hug in return. "See you in the morning."

"'Night, Daddy."

"'Night, ba—" He caught himself just in time. "Good night, Roxie."

"Wait!" She sat up again, and he swallowed frustration and a desperate need for a gin and tonic.

"Yeah?"

"You called Vannie a woman of...what was it?"

"Wisdom," he replied.

"Yeah." She grinned eagerly. "You have to call me something grown-up, too."

He wasn't sure he had a creative thought left in his head tonight.

"Ah...lady of adventure?"

She drew the blankets up to her chin and fell back giggling. "Now say good-night to me again."

He leaned down, a hand on either side of her, and said, "Good night, oh lady of adventure."

She looked pleased. "Good night, Daddy."

He flipped off her light and pulled her door halfway closed. Then he backtracked to peer inside the guest room and found Natalie Browning still fast asleep, Starla clutched in her arms.

Her left leg, though, had kicked free of the blankets and now dangled over the side, covered in goose bumps from the cold. Ben groaned and went to his room for a pair of thermal underwear bottoms he wore when he worked outdoors in winter.

He carried them back to her room, wondering if he had the courage to put them on her. She was huddled under the covers as though cold, and he decided that he could be clinical about this in the interest of her welfare.

With swift but careful movements, he slipped the left leg of the longies over her foot, pushed the blankets aside to find her other foot and pulled the other leg on.

He almost hesitated when it came to slipping them over her hips but knew the less he thought about it, the better. He simply leaned over her with an arm under her waist, held her to him for the time it took to pull them over her bottom, then almost gasped with relief when he could lay her down again. He covered her quickly and left the room.

He went downstairs feeling as though the day had been thirty hours long. He mixed a gin and tonic, sat down on a bright red sofa he'd bought because the girls loved it, and propped his feet up on an old wooden garden bench he'd cleaned up and brought inside.

He turned on the Home and Garden Channel, hoping Norm Abrams was sharing an interesting building project. Ben leaned his head against the high cushions and let his eyes drift closed during a commercial about waterproof stain.

He was asleep before the commercial was over.

NATALIE AWOKE TO a headache so brutal she dared not open her eyes.

I'm having a stroke! she thought in panic. *Or I've been struck on the head with something heavy! I've been mugged!*

Mugged. No. The warm cocoon in which she was wrapped didn't feel very post-mugging.

And she probably wasn't having a stroke. She could move her arm, flex her fingers, put them to her head, where there was no evidence of a bump or a cut. So she hadn't been struck, either.

She tried hard to think, but her aching head made it almost impossible.

Then she realized she could hardly breathe and her throat was scratchy. The cold. She had an awful cold. She'd taken two cold tablets, then two more, then someone had given her a powerful brandy drink....

Suddenly it all came back. The sperm bank, her investigation and KXAV's humiliating report, followed by her starring role in Jolie Ramirez's "Celebrity Dish." There'd been the trip to Dancer's Beach and Dori's absence, the lowest moment of Natalie's life.

Her head thudded viciously in response to her brain activity, and she was forced to give it a rest.

I'm hungover, she thought defeatedly. She wasn't

hurt or ill; she was hungover on cold medication and brandy. She vaguely remembered still feeling poorly after the drink and taking two more pills. Loggers in spiked boots danced in her head, and she lay quietly for a moment, trying to let her mind rest.

But she had to know things. She had to remember where she was. Her head hurt too much, though, to risk opening her eyes.

She remembered a man and a dog in front of Dori's house, directing her to...the bed-and-breakfast! Yes! She breathed a sigh of relief. Yes. She was on the third floor of a bed-and-breakfast in a pretty brass bed. It was called the Woodsy Cabin Room because there were pine trees and bears and moose on the wallpaper!

She breathed another sigh of relief. There! Her brain was working. She knew where she was. Feeling just a little better about everything, she risked opening her eyes to slits. They encountered bright sunlight and...no pine trees, no bears, no moose.

She sat up, forgetting the state of her head in her sudden panic at the unfamiliar sight of deep, rose-colored walls covered with framed maps and charts and photos of lighthouses.

She was rewarded with a pounding in her head so severe that she put both hands to her ears, certain they were going to fly off from the pressure.

When her head finally quieted, she took another careful look around. Her bed had short, off-center head and footboards in dark wood that suggested she was sleeping on a futon. The dresser was dark wood, and there was a large model of a sailing yacht on the dresser. The yacht was reflected in the mirror behind it so that it looked as though the model and its reflection were in a neck-and-neck race.

In one corner was an upholstered rocking chair in blue and cream; against another wall stood a tall accountant's desk from another century. Her eyes went back to the chair. Her suitcase lay on it.

She sat very still and tried to remember where she was, and how she'd gotten here. But all she could recall was a very fuzzy memory of a man, someone she'd thought had been sent to…impregnate her.

Oh, God! Oh, *God!* She turned to the pillow beside her, wondering if she was sharing the bed with someone she hadn't even noticed in her panic over her strange surroundings.

She emitted a little sound that was half alarm, half amusement at the sight of the two-foot-tall plush bear. One eye had been replaced with a star-shaped piece of felt, and it seemed to wink at her stupidity.

She wished desperately that she could remember what had happened, hoped against hope that she hadn't done anything truly stupid. But she was here, wasn't she? she thought grimly. In a bed she didn't know, in a room that was unfamiliar. Stupid was written all over it.

Well. She tossed the blankets back and carefully put her legs over the side. Her head thumped in response but she ignored it. Her principal priority was to get away before anyone noticed she was awake. If anyone was here.

The clock on the bedside table read just after eight. If she was lucky, whoever owned this home was on the way to work. She studied the bear worriedly for a moment and wondered if it meant there was a child in residence.

She prayed not. She hated to think she'd been out cold in front of a child.

Natalie got as far as the bathroom off the bedroom before she realized what she was wearing. The red-and-black flannel shirt she remembered. But the baggy, waffle-patterned black thermal underwear did not belong to her. Did it?

And if it didn't, who had put it on her? The man she'd thought had come to impregnate her?

With a groan of agony, she fell forward against the door molding and closed her eyes. For a woman who'd once had charge of her destiny, she was making one self-destructive move after another.

After a moment of self-pity, she pushed herself upright again, went into the bathroom, filled the sink with water, found a facecloth and did her best to cat-wash quietly so that if anyone was still around, she could make her escape without disturbing them.

She dug through her bag, found a pair of brown cords and a brown turtleneck sweater, and ran a comb cautiously through her painful hair. She folded the black underwear neatly and left it on the foot of the bed.

Then she opened the door silently and, with suit-case in hand and a blue jeans jacket slung over her arm, tiptoed to the head of a wide stairway. On second thought, she reversed direction and went down a smaller back stairway she hoped would lead to a rear hallway and a back door.

She discovered a moment later that she'd been mistaken. The stairway ended in a bright red-and-white kitchen into which small-paned windows all along one side spilled sunlight.

At a farmer's table in the middle of the room, a man sat reading the paper, while two little girls finished bowls of cereal, their moods apparently morose.

Natalie drew in a breath, distressed at having stumbled into the very confrontation she'd hoped to avoid—and with two beautiful children!

For one instant that would stay with her for a long, long time, she let herself believe that she belonged here, that she'd just showered and dressed and was joining her family for breakfast. The girls were as beautiful as any she'd dreamed of having.

And they looked delighted at the sight of her, grim moods falling away and broad smiles curving their mouths.

"Daddy!" the older of the two girls exclaimed, dark eyes brightening. Natalie guessed her to be seven or eight. "She's awake!"

"Hi!" The second child, probably a couple of years younger, knelt up on her chair in excitement. "My name's Roxie!"

The man looked up from his paper and turned his head in her direction. He had close-cropped, dark brown hair, a strong nose, a square chin with the slightest cleft in it, and a mouth that might have lent that tough face a little softness if it had been smiling.

But it wasn't. And a pair of mahogany-brown eyes said clearly that he disapproved of her.

Time began again and reality descended upon her with a crash.

He was the man in her blurred images of last night. And she'd mentioned impregnation to him; she knew she had. He must think her either a slut or a complete idiot. She didn't really care to know which.

To her utter and complete surprise, he pushed back from the table and stood. "Good morning," he said politely, if a little stiffly.

"Good morning," she replied in a raspy voice. She cleared her throat and smiled at the girls. "Hi. I'm Natalie."

The older girl tried to get up, but the man stopped her with a look. Then he transferred The Look to Natalie. It made her, too, stay in her place.

"I'm Ben Griffin," he said. "My mother owns the bed-and-breakfast where you were staying. These are my daughters, Vanessa and Roxanne."

She smiled at each in turn. Bright smiles that could not be squelched by The Look were offered to her.

"I'm pleased to meet all of you," she said, transferring her suitcase to her other hand. "And I want you to know how grateful I am for your hospitality."

She had a million questions. Had she been rowdy last night and had his mother asked him to get rid of her? Had Natalie invited herself over? Had he invited her after her impregnation remarks?

On second thought, maybe she didn't want her questions answered.

Vanessa turned to her father. "I knew she'd have a nice voice. Does she have to go?"

"Yes, I do," Natalie replied quickly, unwilling to

let Ben Griffin be put on the spot after whatever it was she'd done last night. "I have to…go to work."

"Isn't that in Philadelphia?" he asked.

She wondered how he knew that, then realized that if she'd asked him to impregnate her, chances are she'd told him where she lived. She swallowed a groan.

"Yes. I have to get to the airport."

"I'm afraid we left your car at my mother's," he said. "I'll drive you when I get back from taking the girls to school and day care." He pointed to the bowl at the fourth place set at the table. "Why don't you have some cereal and a cup of coffee, and I'll be back in about fifteen minutes."

"I could take a cab there," she demurred, sure all he needed was to be put to more trouble on her account.

He shook his head. "Cab service died last year."

Roxie, still kneeling on her chair, leaned across the table to shake cereal into the empty bowl. "We really like Frosted Pups. It has colored candies in it, but Daddy says we can't have that except sometimes on Saturdays. It doesn't have enough…" She turned to her sister for help.

"Nutrition," Vanessa enunciated carefully. She pushed the milk in the direction of the empty chair. "Daddy said you could stay for dinner," she added in a rush.

Natalie guessed by the way Ben Griffin stopped in the act of removing a battered suede jacket from the back of his chair that the child had lied.

But he shrugged on the jacket without correcting her.

"That's very generous," Natalie said, beginning to feel his disapproval like a weight and hating that she couldn't respond to the children's warmth. She knew he wouldn't like it. "But I really have to go today."

Both girls looked crestfallen, and she was at a loss to understand their interest in her when she'd hardly spoken to them.

"But I can have breakfast first," she said, hoping to draw back the smiles. She put her suitcase down by the door and went to the table.

Ben poured coffee into her cup, then excused himself to find his car keys.

Vanessa took a napkin from the holder in the middle of the table and walked around to hand it to her. "Would you like a banana for your cereal?" she asked.

Natalie opened the napkin onto her lap. "No, this is fine, thank you. What grade are you in, Vanessa?"

"I'm in second. Roxie's in preschool."

"But I'm gonna get my ears pierced," Roxie said, coming around the table to press in on the other side of Natalie. She put a fingertip to the jade stud in Natalie's closest earlobe. "And I'm gonna get earrings just like yours!"

Vanessa rolled her eyes. "She's not getting her ears pieced until she grows up. Daddy says we're too young. Do you think we're too young?"

"Definitely," she said. "You have to take care of your ears very carefully when you have them pierced or you get an infection. And it's easier to remember all the things you have to do if you're older.''

"How old were you?" Vanessa asked.

"I was in high school," Natalie replied. "My friend gave it to me as a present for my birthday."

"You were sleeping last night," Roxie said, leaning her elbow companionably on the table beside Natalie's bowl and smiling up into her face. "I thought you were Sleeping Beauty! I wanted Daddy to kiss you, but he didn't want to."

Natalie bet he didn't. "I wasn't feeling very well."

Vanessa confirmed that with a nod. "Grandma said you had a cold, then you had some brandy, and you didn't answer the phone."

Natalie propped her elbow on the table and rested her forehead in her hand. It ached abominably.

"Dillydally if you're able," Roxie sang to her, quoting the old aphorism, "but keep your elbows off the table."

Natalie dutifully lowered her elbow.

"That wasn't polite!" Vanessa scolded Roxie. "She's company."

"Daddy says we have to have good table manners all the time!"

"Us, but not her! She's a grown-up!"

"No, no, that's all right." Natalie put an arm around each girl to defuse the argument. "Thank you, Vanessa, but Roxanne is right. Good manners are always important."

Their father returned with a key ring hooked over his index finger. He took in the scene of the three of them and his brow darkened.

Natalie dropped her arms from them and swallowed a lump in her throat as she smiled. "You girls have a good day at school," she said. "And thank you for getting my breakfast together. I'm very glad that I got to meet you."

"You ready, girls?" their father asked.

Vanessa sighed. "Yes. Come on, Roxie."

Vanessa picked up her lunch box from the counter, and Roxie took a well-loved doll from beside her bowl. They stopped to wave as their father held the back door open.

"I'll be right back," he said to Natalie.

The heroic thing to do, she thought, as he closed the door behind him, was to quickly finish her cereal and start walking to the B-and-B. Her suitcase had wheels, and Dancer's Beach was small enough that it would take her only a moment to figure out how to get to the B-and-B from here.

She congratulated herself on the first reasonable plan she'd made since her unfortunate decision to use a sperm bank to get a baby in her life.

She finished her cereal hurriedly, had several sips of hot coffee, then rinsed out her dishes and put them in the sink.

Nothing about the view from the window above the sink looked familiar. She walked into the living room and looked out the large window. She saw that the house was on a hill just above town, and that it was probably six or seven blocks downhill, then just about half a mile to the B-and-B and her car. A cinch. At home she ran three miles every other day.

Unfortunately, she discovered a moment later, she

ran far better than she walked. When she turned to head back to the kitchen to retrieve her suitcase and leave quickly, she caught her foot on a two-by-four in the hallway that she hadn't noticed on her way in. She fell flat on her face, a burning pain ripping through her right ankle.

Chapter Three

Ben dropped Vanessa off at Matthew Buckley School. Children streamed toward the building from all directions.

"I think you should ask her to stay for dinner," Vanessa said as she leaned over to kiss him goodbye. "I think she's very nice. It isn't her fault that she couldn't wake up and Grandma had to make her leave 'cause she'd promised her room to somebody else."

All he needed at this point in his life, Ben thought, was a ditzy blonde with eyes like those of a silent-film star, all anguish and repentance. Life was hard, but you had to behave with some common sense and resist being splashed all over the news. Even if you were beautiful.

"You heard her, Van," he replied. "She has to go home."

"That's 'cause she knows you don't like her."

"I don't even know her." He tried to plead innocence.

"You look at her the same way you look at us when we do something we're not supposed to do."

"But it doesn't mean I don't like you, does it?"

he challenged. "It just means I want you to do the right thing."

"Yeah, but she doesn't know you like we do," his daughter explained patiently. "She probably thinks you don't like her."

She was so much like her mother. "Will you please go to school?" He pinched her nose and unlocked her door. "I love you."

"I love you, too," she said, but grudgingly.

Roxie was silent all the way to the day care. He'd have probably gotten the same treatment from her before she got out of the car, except that Marianne came to open her door. She was tall and angular with a long dark braid and soft hazel eyes that devoured him every time she looked at him.

To his recollection, he'd never done anything to encourage her, but she'd either misinterpreted something he'd said or done, or she was simply determined to lust him into submission.

She leaned into the car as Roxie darted off to join her friends. "Good morning, Ben," she said. With the children, she had a loud, high-pitched voice. With him, it dropped an octave and was little more than an intimate whisper.

"Good morning," he replied, putting a briskness into the greeting so that she couldn't misinterpret it.

"The Butlers and the Kaminskis think you'd be a wonderful addition to the board," she said. "Are you sure I can't *persuade* you to reconsider?"

The implication was in the subtle inflection. He kept his smile brisk, too. "Nope, sorry. Too much to do."

Her expression became sympathetic. He mistrusted that almost as much as the direct come-on. "I know. Single fathers have such a tough road. Hopefully, the right woman will come along very soon."

The right woman had gone, but he kept that to himself. "I'm pretty determined to go it alone. But thanks for your concern."

She apparently hadn't heard him. "She could be right under your nose," she suggested.

Mercifully, his cell phone rang. "Excuse me," he said, turning the key in the ignition, then picking up his phone and flipping it open. He backed out of the driveway as he answered, Marianne staring wistfully after him.

"Ben, it's Mom."

"Hi, Mom."

"How's Natalie this morning?"

"Fine. Having cereal. We're coming by in a little bit to pick up her car."

There was an aggravated sigh on the other end of the connection. "Ben Griffin, I swear. Life drops a beautiful woman right into your lap, and you send her packing."

He shook his head at the road. "Life didn't drop her, Mom, you did. And it's not going to work, so cut it out, all right? You want anything from the bakery on my way to your place?"

"Don't try to soft-soap me with promises of pastry," she said with affronted dignity.

"Okay. I'll see you in about fifteen minutes."

"Ben!"

"Yeah?"

"An apple fritter. A big one."

"You got it."

All right, Ben thought. He was the one in control. He had to fight every moment to maintain it, but right now, he was in charge.

OR SO HE THOUGHT.

When he walked into the house, the table was cleared and Natalie's dishes were in the sink. But there was no sign of her. Her suitcase was where she'd placed it when she sat down to breakfast.

Maybe she was freshening up, he thought.

He was halfway to the coffeepot with his commuter mug when he heard a faint voice from the direction of the living room.

"Ben?" it called. "Is that you?"

He was touched by an unsettling foreboding. Was that Natalie?

He followed the sound, then stopped in his tracks at the sight of her lying on the carpet, propped up on an elbow, her face pale, her mouth tight. The two-by-four he'd brought up from the basement that morning to remind himself to fix the front porch railing had been flipped over and lay partially under her.

No, he thought firmly. *This is not happening to me.*

He dropped to his knees beside her and saw that her left ankle was purple and already several times its normal size.

"I think it's just a sprain," she said heavily. "But I can't get up. If you can help me and just take me to my car..." Then she added mournfully, "I'm sorry. I didn't see the lumber."

It was his fault, but he wanted to blame her. "What were you doing in here, anyway?" he demanded.

She nodded as though she'd expected that accusing question. "I was determined to walk to town so you wouldn't have to drive me, so I came to look out the window to sort of orient myself. I'm sorry. I know I've just made everything worse. But if you can just get me to my car, I'll be fine."

"Right. Like I would do that." He had no reason to bark at her, but it helped relieve the anger he felt that she couldn't just walk out of his life this morning as he'd hoped. As he needed. And it was all his fault.

He slipped an arm between her propped elbow and her side, then one rather familiarly under her hips.

She wrapped her arms instinctively around his neck. "I can hop if you'll give me a little support."

He ignored her and brought himself to a standing position without losing her. He strode through the house and out to the van, though she had to open doors.

He put her in the middle seat in the back, so that he could prop up her foot. He handled it carefully, placing it on a pillow he kept for the girls. Then he looked up at her to ask if that was comfortable.

She looked pale and miserable.

His anger evaporated. "I'll take you to the clinic to make sure you didn't break anything." He put a plaid blanket with a fleece lining over her. "Just lie quietly. We'll be there in five minutes."

She lay back with a groan. "I'm sorry," she said again. "I *hate* this."

Yeah, me, too, he thought silently.

"I know you hate it, too," she said for him. "I meant to be less trouble and ended up being more. I don't seem to be able to make a right move lately."

"I've had my share of those days," he consoled her. "Just relax."

She was quiet as he drove down the hill and headed up Beach Avenue toward the clinic.

"Was I...causing a scene last night at your mother's?" she asked, her voice sounding stiff and choked.

He decided she could use a break. "No," he replied. "She called me because you wouldn't answer her knock, and she knew you hadn't eaten. She was worried about you."

"I was probably sleeping. I've had a difficult couple of weeks and I haven't slept very well. Then I was taking pills and she gave me that toddy...."

"She had other guests coming in last night to whom she'd promised the room, so she had to...remove you."

The silence was thick for a moment. He could hear her sorting through words for the right thing to say. Then she uttered a little sound of exasperation and blurted, "There's just no subtle way to ask this."

He couldn't see her in the rearview mirror because she was lying down. He had the weirdest sensation that he was having a conversation with an invisible woman.

"Ask what?"

There was another heavy pause, then another abrupt question. "Did I say anything to you about...?" She stopped as though it was just too hard, after all, then seemed to reconsider and began again. "Did I ask you if you'd been sent to impregnate me?"

He had to admire her willingness to confront an uncomfortable situation head-on.

"Yes, you did," he answered. Then he decided he could give her another break. "Of course, I was confused, but after you passed out and my mother was packing up your things, we saw the newspaper. It explained some."

Natalie groaned aloud, a muffled sound that suggested her hands were probably over her face. "I'm so sorry," she said. "I'm usually the epitome of decorum, but then I don't usually drink. I guess that little bit of brandy made me more direct than it's safe to be. I apologize if I offended you."

He turned into the clinic parking lot. "I'm a builder who's spent most of his time working in the company of other men. I'm not offendable."

"But your girls are so sweet," she said, a trace of self-loathing in her voice, "and I can tell by the way you are with them that you're trying to provide a gentle, protective upbringing, and here I'm pushed into your life, trying to compromise you before I even know your name, then passing out cold."

He parked in a spot near the door and hurried around to the passenger side. He slid the van door open and found her sitting up, her face blotchy, her eyes grim.

"I didn't tell them that part," he said with a reluctant grin. "And they just thought you were asleep." He placed a knee on the edge of the floor and managed to lift her off the seat and out of the van.

"Well...I'm sorry."

"You can stop saying that." He bounced her once in his arms to firm his grip on her, then carried her inside. "If it's anyone's fault that you fell, it's mine."

"I'm not talking about falling." She lowered her voice as they walked into the cool, quiet office. "I'm talking about..."

"You're talking *too much.*" He whispered the last two words as a woman in a lab coat came out from an inner office.

She took one look at Natalie's ankle and waved him back into one of only three examining rooms.

Dr. Greg Fortuna, a man about Ben's age who'd given the girls their back-to-school inoculations, bustled into the room, frowning solicitously over Natalie's injury.

He'd been in Dancer's Beach less than a year, but he was well liked and respected. Ben had worked with him on a volunteer committee for the men's mission and considered him a friend. Vanessa thought he looked like Antonio Sabato, Jr.

"Greg Fortuna," he said, shaking Natalie's hand. "Hi, Ben. Did you mow this poor woman down?"

"I fell over a two-by-four," Natalie explained.

"Oh. You working with Ben?"

"No, this was in his living room," she replied. Then she seemed to doubt the wisdom of admitting that—as though thinking that Ben expected discretion—and she turned to him, looking stricken.

He wondered absently what her life had been like that she second-guessed every word and every move. It was clear from what she'd said and from the newspaper article that the last two weeks had been difficult, but this self-doubt seemed to be of long standing.

"She's visiting from Philadelphia," Ben said. "She stayed at Mom's, then Mom ran out of room, so the girls invited her to stay overnight with us."

Natalie looked grateful for the slightly fictitious intervention.

"Looks like just a sprain," Greg said, "but we'll x-ray it to be sure. Just sit tight, Natalie, and we'll wheel you right into the lab." He turned to Ben, uncertain of their relationship despite his careful explanation. "You coming?"

Ben picked up a copy of *Popular Mechanics* from a small table in the corner. "I'll wait right here."

"Good enough."

Ben was just getting into an article about winterizing outdoor pipes when his cell phone rang.

"Bijou Development," he answered, tapping his pockets for a pen.

"Henrietta Caldwell said she saw you carrying a woman into the van!" his mother said, not bothering with a greeting. "Is Natalie Browning *still* asleep?"

Henrietta Caldwell lived across the road and was one of his mother's church cronies. He suspected she'd reported on him before.

"And how did Mrs. Caldwell happen to observe this?" he asked, closing the magazine.

"It was perfectly innocent," his mother replied defensively. "Her husband has this telescope set up in the attic...."

"Yeah. And there are so many stars out at eight-thirty in the morning."

There was a huff of dismay, then a testy, "Are you going to tell me if she's all right or not?"

"She's going to be fine," he replied, tossing the magazine back on the table, knowing his momentary respite from the women in his life was over. "But she did fall in the living room and sprain her ankle. At least Greg thinks it's just a sprain."

"Are you at the clinic?"

"Yes."

"I'll be right over."

"Mom..."

"Breakfast is over and all my guests have scattered. I'll be right there."

She hung up without giving him another chance to protest.

She arrived before Greg returned with Natalie from the lab. Lulu was wearing fuchsia and looked as though she belonged on the cover of some fashion magazine for senior women.

"If you were any kind of gentleman," she accused, taking the doctor's chair from behind the small desk and rolling it beside his, "you'd have caught her before she fell."

"I was taking the girls to school," he replied calmly, determined not to let her exasperate him. She usually did it so successfully.

"Did she trip?"

"Over a two-by-four."

"You couldn't have bought a house that was already fixed?"

"I'm a builder, Mom. Fixing houses and buildings or putting them up is what I do."

"And now you've probably broken the leg of the woman God dropped in your lap."

"It's sprained, not broken," he said evenly. "And you dropped her, not God. Not the fates. You."

"Why didn't you call me?"

"Because it just happened. I rushed her right over here, but I'd have called you when I got home."

"With a little warning I could have brought a casserole."

"For what? To use as a poultice? Greg's taking good care of her."

She gave him a lethal look. "So that you don't have to cook tonight. You'll have enough on your hands with an invalid."

He'd opened his mouth to repeat that it was probably just a sprain and that the invalid was very determined to go home when Greg wheeled Natalie back into the examining room. On Natalie's left leg was a fat Ace bandage wrapped under her foot and around her leg. On top of it was an ice pack.

"Always pays to be sure," Greg said. "It's just a sprain. She should stay off it for a couple of days. The thing to remember is RICE."

Ben blinked at him. "Pardon me?"

"RICE," Greg repeated, ticking the items off on his fingers. "Rest. Ice. Compression—that's the bandage. Elevation. Keep it up."

Ben nodded. "Got you."

To someone else, Natalie might have looked cheerful and in control, but Ben knew what it was like to feel one thing and project another for the comfort of those around you. Under the facade, she was on the brink of tears.

"Don't worry," she said to him, with a smiling glance at his mother. "I'm sure I can find someone to drive me to the airport."

Greg frowned. "I think it'll be tough negotiating the airport with that ankle if you're traveling alone. There are wheelchairs, but what about stowing your carry-ons, up and down the aisle to the rest room? It's not as though Portland to Philadelphia is a one-hour flight. People in wheelchairs usually travel with someone to handle the details. If your trip can wait a few days, I think that would be advisable."

"When you arrived," Lulu said, "you told me you didn't have to be back to work for a month, that you were waiting for your cousin to return from a trip and intended to spend a little time with her. And didn't you hear what the doctor said? RICE!"

Natalie studied Lulu uncertainly.

"Natalie, this is my mother, Louise Griffin," Ben explained. "She runs the B-and-B."

"Of course." Natalie smiled apologetically. "I'm so sorry I was a problem."

His mother shook her head. "You weren't. I'd just promised the room and I couldn't wake you up. So, you don't *have* to go home, do you?"

Ben didn't understand why he could read Natalie's mind so clearly, but he could. She wasn't at all like him, and yet he seemed to relate to her in some way he didn't understand.

She felt cornered by her situation. She'd been cornered one time too many and was determined that it wasn't going to happen again. But she had no idea how to fight it.

"You'll stay with us," he said, getting to his feet,

reaching for her jacket on the simple wire rack in the corner, "at least until you can move around more comfortably."

He'd learned from his daughters that when he wanted cooperation, he never posed a question, but always made a statement. "You will..." always got much better results than "Do you want to...?"

He turned to Greg for corroboration.

"A much more sensible plan," he praised. "And it's going to hurt for a few days." He handed Ben a prescription. "One every eight hours or as needed. If there's any problem, call me."

Lulu took the prescription from him. "I'll pick it up while you take her home."

Natalie looked as though she'd have happily had the leg removed rather than return with Ben.

Without giving her time to think, he thanked Greg, then scooped her up again and left the office.

She borrowed his cell phone on the way home and tried her cousin's number.

He stopped at a light and she handed the phone back, her eyes miserable. She'd gotten no answer.

"You're sure there's not a motel or a boarding-house?" she pleaded.

He shook his head as he placed the phone on the console between them. "It'll be all right. The girls will be thrilled. Remember how badly they wanted you to stay for dinner? Imagine how happy they'll be when you tell them you're staying for a couple of days."

"But you're not happy."

"Is that important?"

She dropped her head against the rest and closed

her eyes. "If you're willing to extend your hospitality, I guess it isn't. But I hate it when people don't like me. I'm a people pleaser by nature, you know? I get lots of positive mail on my job, but I'll worry about that one viewer who thinks I'm stiff or unappealing."

"I don't think you're unappealing," he said, wanting her to feel less distress without letting her think he was looking forward to the next few days. He wasn't. For reasons he couldn't explain, it hurt almost physically to look at her.

They were almost home when she asked quietly, "Are you widowed or divorced?"

"My wife died of a stroke a year and a half ago," he said. It hurt to say the words, just as it always did. But he made himself tell the whole story. "She was a decorator working on one of the new homes on the cove. She'd complained of a headache that morning. I gave her a neck rub, then went off to work. She took the girls to school, went to the job and collapsed there in the middle of the morning. She was gone when the ambulance arrived."

He slowed to turn onto his street, and saw that she was staring at him, her eyes brimming with his pain as well as hers.

"How did you go on?"

"Reluctantly at first," he admitted. "We'd been friends since high school, so I lost my best buddy as well as my wife. Then Vanessa couldn't stop crying, and Roxie wouldn't stop asking where Julie was, so I knew I had to take control of her death before it controlled me, and therefore, them. So I had to make it clear to Roxie that she wasn't coming back, make sure Vanessa understood that it was hideous,. but it wasn't the end of the world, then I somehow had to believe it myself."

He turned into the driveway, braked and turned off the motor. They sat in silence for a moment.

"And do you?" she asked.

"When I'm strong," he replied candidly. "But when everything's going wrong, or the girls are cranky, or the house is quiet on a Sunday morning, I feel as though I've died, too."

"I didn't know her," Natalie said, "but judging by how wonderful your girls are and how much you love her, I imagine she'd hate knowing you feel that way."

He nodded. "That's why I keep trying."

He climbed out of the van and walked around to open her door. He tried not to think about how many times he was going to have to take her in his arms over the next few days. She was soft and fragrant and had a tendency to wrap her arms around him in a trusting way that unsettled him.

He had a building to restore, a house to remodel, a recalcitrant mother to keep happy and two daughters to raise.

He didn't need a beautiful single woman in his life, prodding his libido awake and forcing him to deal with whether or not he was ready to close Julie away.

Then...why had he invited Natalie to stay with him?

Chapter Four

Natalie wrapped her arms around Ben's neck as he carried her into the house. Part of her was numb with embarrassment and guilt at the trouble she'd caused herself and him. But another part of her was awakening to the discomfort in her leg, and she wanted nothing more than to melt into a quiet corner somewhere.

Ben stopped in the middle of the living room.

"Will you be comfortable in what you're wearing?" he asked. "Or did you bring something more appropriate for lying on the sofa for a few days?"

"I did bring sweatshirts," she replied wearily, "but only jeans for pants, and I doubt that the leg will fit over my bandage."

He nodded. "What about the thermal underwear I put you in last night? It's not very fashionable, but when you're covered with a blanket, no one will notice."

That sounded reasonable. "And I doubt I'll be getting much company."

"All right." He carried her upstairs and placed her on the futon she'd used last night. "I'll go back down for your bag, then I'll get a pair of those longies for you."

"Thank you."

She heard his quick footsteps as he went down the stairs, then up again. He opened the suitcase on the mattress beside her so that she could dig out a sweat-shirt, then disappeared again.

He was back in a moment with a pair of long underwear bottoms that were thermal and black, but silky.

"Whoa," she said as he handed them to her. They were wonderfully soft to the touch. "I didn't realize builders were into such decadent comfort."

He rolled his eyes. "They were a gift from my mother. I thought they were a little much when she gave them to me, but they feel wonderful. Working outdoors in the winter can be very miserable, so it helps if you're at least comfortable in your own clothes."

She could relate to that. "The first year I was a reporter," she said, digging to the bottom of the case for a simple, dark blue sweatshirt, "I got all the worst assignments. It was a banner year for snow and I re-ported it from all over the eastern seaboard. I could have used a pair of these then. Ah! Here it is!"

"How long ago was that?"

"Four years." She closed the top of her case. "Then somebody in power decided I had audience appeal, and I got the Sunday anchor spot, then even-tually, weekday evenings."

"You had a fast-moving career."

She shrugged. "It's not national television. And it's

just because I have a face that appears sincere. The viewing audience likes someone they can believe in.'' She smiled in sudden self-deprecation. ''They don't know that I mix cold medication and brandy and can totally upset a small town.''

His smile was barely there. ''Well, in the interest of your career, we'll keep our secret.'' He gestured toward her shirt. ''Can you manage all right?''

She nodded firmly. ''I'm sure I can.''

''Okay.'' He backed toward the door. ''Shout for me when you're ready to come down. I'll close the door, but I won't latch it.''

''Will you hear me from downstairs?''

''Sure. My ear's attuned to listening for the girls. I can hear a rag doll drop when the television's on.'' He walked out of the room and pulled the door most of the way shut.

When she heard him go down the stairs, she drew the first calm breath she'd taken since he'd arrived home that morning and found her on the floor.

She pulled the brown turtleneck over her head and quickly drew on the sweatshirt. She sneezed, dabbed at her nose with a tissue, then lay back to unbutton and unzip the cords and push them down past her hips. She sat up again and got her free leg out of them, then struggled a little to get them past her bandage.

She got her free leg into the silky longies, then struggled a little with the second leg. Finally pulling them into place, she dug into her bag for her sewing kit, pulled out a large safety pin and fastened several inches of the too-large waistband over itself.

Drawing a steadying breath, she shouted Ben's name.

He was there in an instant, looking as though he carried women around the house every day.

His brisk manner should have negated her embarrassment, and it might have had she not remembered—even vaguely—the things she'd said to him while intoxicated.

"I'm ready," she said, then remembered to grab her box of tissues and clutch it in one arm. As he lifted her, she wrapped the other arm around his neck.

She was struck anew by what a handsome man he was. It was hard to believe that slender Lulu Griffin had produced such a tall, well-built son.

"What did your father do?" she asked as he walked sideways out the door with her. She was very much aware of the muscular arm around her back and the other holding tightly to her thighs. She was desperate for distracting conversation.

"He was a judge." Ben went easily down the stairs. "In family court. He was a little conservative, a little stuffy, but he agonized over his decisions and was a very good human being." He laughed lightly, even a little sadly. "I don't know why he and my mother found each other appealing. I mean, they were both attractive, wonderful people, but they had nothing in common that I could see. My father just did everything she wanted without ever really understanding her, I think."

"Were they happy?"

"They seemed to be, but I always thought they

could never really tap into all they could do for each other because they were so different.''

He put her on the sofa at the edge of the kitchen and covered her with an afghan of colorful crocheted granny squares.

"Did your mother make this?" Natalie asked.

He shook his head as he tugged the blanket down over her feet. "Julie's mom. Geez! Your feet are frozen. Hold on.''

He disappeared into a room off the kitchen she guessed might be the laundry room and returned with a pair of thick gray socks. He sat on the far corner of the sofa, lifted her feet into his lap and worked the socks on to them.

"Mom's not into needlework. Julie's mother made it.''

"Does she live here?"

"Florida. Her husband's gone, but her two sisters are there. Do you still have your parents?"

"My mother." She hesitated, never knowing how to explain her. "She means well, but she's your classic control freak. An opinionated control freak.''

He gave her a smiling glance as he got the sock in place on her good foot and pulled the top halfway up to her knee. "Then she has a lot in common with my mother.''

Natalie smiled politely in return, certain Letitia Browning had little in common with anyone, unless Attila the Hun had a sister.

"Maybe you should call her," he suggested as he opened the second sock widely in his hands to fit it over her bandaged ankle. "I'll get you the cordless phone to keep nearby this afternoon. I've got to go to work for a while.''

"I'll be fine," she insisted. "And I think I'll leave the call to my mother until I'm on my way home. She's very conscious of how things look, what people think, and she was very traumatized over the whole sperm bank scandal. Knowing I passed out cold in a very respectable B-and-B and am now in temporary cohabitation with a single man would be the final straw for her.''

The sock in place, he absently rubbed her feet. "Then just remind yourself that you did the best you could under difficult circumstances and what anyone else thinks—including your mother—doesn't really matter.''

She nodded. "I know that's true, but it's one of those things that's easy for someone else to tell you, but hard to put into practice. My mother's a formidable woman and I've always disappointed her. Still, I find myself hoping for approval.''

"Yeah, well, I guess that's just human nature. So, was she against the sperm bank thing?''

Natalie felt herself relaxing just a little after the difficult morning. "She wanted me to go to Genius Labs.''

"Who?''

"Genius Labs. It's a lab that specializes in extremely high IQs, particularly in the sciences. But I love the arts and thought a child might be happier with the gift of music or painting. She thought that was foolish when I had the opportunity to guarantee a brilliant income as well as a brilliant child.''

"Then she disapproved. And was probably happy to tell you that when it all fell apart."

"Yes, indeed."

"You must have guessed that would happen when you did the story."

She nodded fatalistically. "I've blown other phases of my life, but I'm a good reporter. When I realized what was going on, I decided that I would tell the story no matter how it affected me. I had to stop him from hurting anyone else."

"How old are you?" he asked.

She blinked, surprised by the sudden turn in the conversation. "Twenty-six," she answered.

He seemed to puzzle over that. "Can I be candid?" he asked. "Possibly even rude, though that's not my intention?"

She didn't think there was anything in the world that could still hurt her feelings. "Why not?" She grinned. "I am wearing your underwear, after all."

He didn't seem to notice the joke. "Why," he asked quietly, "would a beautiful young woman like you, not even yet in her prime, go to a sperm bank for a baby when you haven't even given yourself the chance to meet the right man?"

That was the question everyone asked. That was why she tried for the most part to keep the decision to herself.

"If you knew Julie in high school," she explained quietly, "it's probably hard for you to understand the loneliness of the singles scene. I don't drink as a rule. I don't care if other people want to, I'm just not comfortable in a bar. I went to a lot of social events because tickets to everything in town circulate through the television studios. But every man there knew me as the face on television and either wanted something from me publicitywise, or wanted to be seen with me for some imagined status. Then I met Kyle Wagner at a party and thought I'd found the perfect man. He was kind, attentive, interesting.''

''What did he do?''

''He was an actor.''

When Ben looked skeptical, she shook her head. ''No, that was a good thing. It takes someone else in the entertainment business to understand the hours required in pursuit of the news.''

''Then what happened?''

She frowned, still remembering the surprise she'd felt when she'd realized he didn't love her at all. ''We were engaged and I just realized one day that he didn't love me the way a life partner should love the other. I tried to think of him first, consult him before making decisions that affected both of us, tried to accommodate whatever it was he wanted to do.''

''And he didn't do that.''

''No. Then he told me he didn't want children until he was forty. It took a visit to my cousin Dori's to see how her husband treated her, how he looked at her, how much he loved their child, for me to realize that I'd never be happy with less than that.''

''But why the sperm bank?''

''Because I think even more than a husband,'' she said with a what-can-you-do splay of her hands, ''I wanted a baby. And I almost settled for Kyle because I thought he would provide me with one. Then Dori said teasingly that I should think about having a baby without a man involved. And the answer was the sperm bank.''

Ben looked not so much disapproving as disbelieving, but he said nothing.

She drew a deep breath. "But, in one of those dirty little tricks life plays on you once in a while, I wasn't able to get pregnant. Even under perfect laboratory conditions, it just wouldn't take. So my fertility specialist suggested we try a second time because he couldn't find a problem with me and concluded it must have been the sperm. It was when he had the second round from another donor tested because I still wasn't conceiving that we discovered that the DNA was precisely the same, though the lab had given us two different donor profiles.''

"But there's nothing wrong with your reproductive system?"

"Not according to my doctor. So I don't know how to explain it. Unless it's stress or something. Or I want it so badly I'm somehow sabotaging myself.''

He propped an elbow on the back of the sofa and nodded consideringly. "I suppose that's possible. There's a lot more involved than simply the physical contact of sperm and egg.''

"This was a lab," she reminded him. "Optimum conditions.''

A line appeared between his eyes. "Hardly optimum. If you had a husband holding your hand, maybe, and you were both sharing everything, but…''

She was always in the forefront of the defense of new medical procedures that many people dismissed as sterile. "It's an amazing breakthrough. Thousands of women who'd never be able to conceive, can now...."

He leaned toward her slightly. "But you're not one of them," he said. "Your body's working."

"Then why aren't I pregnant?"

"Because those procedures are the answer for those who have no alternative. But otherwise, a baby should not be planted in your body in a lab. It should come about as a result of love so strong between two people that it requires a third person to help hold it all."

She felt pinned in place by his words. They simply didn't apply to her, but there was comfort in knowing a man who felt that way.

"Vanessa was the result of Julie and I being so much in love we couldn't keep our hands off each other. She came two months before our first anniversary." He smiled wistfully as he spoke. "Roxie came because we'd argued over whether or not Julie should take a job that would require she be in San Francisco for a month. I didn't want her to go, and she thought she should. I finally realized I was being selfish and apologized." His gaze was unfocused now, seeing another time, another woman. "It earned me a night I can still feel if I close my eyes."

How strong was a love that was still felt, rather than just remembered, six years later? Natalie wondered jealously.

"Well, that's all well and good," she said, restlessly moving her good foot and bringing him back to the present, "but some of us don't have undying love relationships. And I was hoping I didn't have to be deprived of a child because of it.''

He stood, looking weary suddenly. ''I'm sure you don't. The rules just don't work for everyone.''

That intimate and rather heavy conversation was abruptly terminated when there was a light rap on the back door, followed by the entrance of Ben's mother. She carried two white bags, one with the name of a pharmacy and the other with the name of a bakery.

''I'm sorry it took so long,'' she apologized, ''but I thought I'd bring us back something for coffee break. Can I invite myself?''

''If you make the coffee,'' Ben said. ''It's a great idea. I have to reschedule a couple of things for this afternoon, if you ladies will excuse me for a minute.''

Lulu shooed him away. ''But don't be too long or I'll show Natalie your naked baby pictures. Natalie, orange-cranberry muffin, apple fritter or maple bar?''

''Um…what's your preference?''

''I'm addicted to fritters,'' Lulu admitted.

''And Ben's?''

''He's not into sweets like I am.''

Natalie made a face. ''He'd rather have the muffin than the maple bar?''

''Sad but true.'' Lulu went to a corner where there was a stack of nesting snack tables, and brought the larger one to place beside the sofa. She put a dark blue place mat on it, then brought Natalie a glass of water and the bottle of pain medication.

''I feel responsible for this happening to you,'' she said apologetically as Natalie downed the pill.

Natalie handed back the glass and frowned at her. "Whatever for?"

"Because I had to get you out of the Woodsy Cabin Room and that's the reason you're here."

"Oh, please, Lulu. I can't believe I did such a stupid thing as get myself into such a state that I had to be physically moved from place to place by someone else. I'm sorry to have embarrassed and inconvenienced you."

Lulu patted her shoulder. "Nonsense. It takes a lot more than that to embarrass me. And I was more concerned than inconvenienced. Fortunately, Ben was able to help me."

"He's been very kind," Natalie said, leaving nothing in her voice or manner to suggest that he was also, however gently, judgmental and disapproving.

Lulu put the glass in the sink and went about preparing coffee and taking down cups and plates. "He's a little bit of a stuffed shirt sometimes, but he's like his father was—as honest as the day is long and, when he's on your side, as loyal a friend as you'd ever hope to find."

"You're sure there isn't someplace else in town that rents rooms?" Natalie asked, feeling even more guilty. "I hate to put him out any more than I've already done."

"There isn't," Lulu insisted. "And he doesn't mind."

Natalie didn't want to argue that. She knew he did mind, but Lulu was trying so hard to make her feel welcome that she didn't want to do anything to suggest that she wasn't appreciative.

"Vanessa and Roxie are wonderful." Natalie leaned back against her pillows and sniffed the air as the aroma of coffee began to fill the room. "You can see how loved they are."

Lulu took a napkin from the middle of the kitchen table and placed it and a fork on Natalie's little tray table. "The girls were Ben's and Julie's whole world, and now that Julie's gone, Ben stretches himself in every direction, hoping, I think, that he can stop them from feeling the loss."

"Yes." Natalie pulled her blanket up as she watched Lulu move around the kitchen. "He told me how he had to make himself get it together after she died because the girls were suffering."

Lulu turned away from the counter to face her. "Did he? Well. That's a good sign."

Natalie didn't understand that. "A sign of what?"

"Of...loosening up, I guess. He thinks he has to present an image of being impervious to pain, invincible, the man with all the answers." She went to the refrigerator and pulled out a carton of milk, pouring a small amount into a cream pitcher. "But you can't fall in love unless you're vulnerable."

"Does he want to get married again?"

Lulu sent Natalie a sly glance as she put back the milk. "I don't think so. But I want him to. The girls should have a mother, and he's too fine a man to be wasted on bachelorhood."

Natalie leaned her elbow on her pillow and her head on her hand. "He sounded as though he intends to love Julie forever."

"That's fine," Lulu said with a philosophical shrug

as she crossed the kitchen again. "But there's a limit to how much she can do for him at this point. And I won't rest until he starts going out again and seeing a flesh-and-blood woman."

"Then you're going to be awake for a long, long time," Ben said, striding into the kitchen and putting his cell phone on the table. He glanced at Natalie with a grin. "Watch yourself. Now that she knows you're lying there, helpless, she'll probably arrange for a parade of eligible Dancer's Beach bachelors to file through."

Natalie laughed lightly. "Do you know any who like horror movies and dancing?" she asked as Lulu brought her the maple bar and a cup of coffee.

Natalie tried to push herself to a sitting position.

Without warning, a pair of male arms reached under hers and pulled until she sat up. "How's that?" he asked, looking her over as though assessing for himself how she was.

"Fine," she said breathlessly, feeling as though everything inside her had stalled.

He walked off into the living room and her breath returned in a rush, only to halt again as he stuffed a fat pillow between her back and the soft bed pillow.

"Aren't those incompatible preferences?" he asked, stepping back to look her over again. "Better?"

"Yes, thank you," she said, her voice a little loud in her attempt to find it at all. She made a conscious effort to lower it. "Is what incompatible?"

"Dancing and horror movies."

"*I* like them both."

"Women are allowed to be quirky," he said. "Guys go for a more even image." Then he pulled out a chair at the table for his mother, and Natalie felt something inside her melt.

"Then which would you prefer?" she asked after a moment.

"You need cream or sugar?" he asked.

"Cream, please."

He brought the pitcher to her and let her serve herself.

"One of my favorite movies," he said as he reclaimed the pitcher, "is *Lake Placid.*"

She gasped in surprise. The witty horror film about a giant crocodile in a lake in Maine was one of her favorites, too. "I love that movie!" she exclaimed.

"I have it on tape." He went back to the table and handed his mother the pitcher. "I'll move the television in here so you can watch it. But not when the girls are around. Vanessa cries over *The Lion King.*"

Natalie considered that detail about him surprising. Kyle had thought horror movies silly and a waste of time. She'd always thought they were fun because they frightened you but posed no real threat because the scenario was usually fantastical.

The conversation continued for the half hour they spent over morning coffee. The sofa Natalie occupied was situated at the edge of the kitchen, so she was comfortably included in the conversation about the goings-on in Dancer's Beach, and the two empty shops Ben was remodeling in the Bijou Theater Building.

"I have to go to work," Ben said finally, gathering

up her cup and plate as his mother cleared the table. "But I'll be back in time to fix you some lunch."

"Oh, please don't," Natalie implored. "After the maple bar, I'll be fine until dinner. Don't make a special trip home. I'll just sleep all afternoon."

"I have to go home and do laundry," Lulu said to Ben, "but I'll look in on her this afternoon. Don't worry. And I'll bring a casserole for dinner. You want a ride to my house to drive her rental car back? Or return it?"

"What's your preference?" Ben asked Natalie. "Shall I return it for you? I'm sure we can find you a ride to the airport when the time comes."

That was probably the sensible thing to do. "Yes. Take it back, please. I'd appreciate that. If you'll get me my purse..."

He shook his head. "I'll take care of it and we'll square up later." He put the cordless phone on Natalie's small table and dropped his business card beside it. "If you need something, call."

She wouldn't, but she nodded obligingly.

"Your crutches are right here." He pointed to them with the toe of his boot. They lay against the bottom of the sofa. "And don't be overconfident with them. I've used them and it takes a while to adjust to them."

She nodded. "I'll be careful."

She basked in his solicitousness, then realized he probably didn't want her to injure her good leg and have to stay longer.

The moment Ben and Lulu were out the door, Natalie sank into her pillows, relieved to be alone at last. She appreciated their care and attention, but she couldn't help feeling guilty about the time it took away from their busy workdays.

And the fact was she could breathe more evenly when Ben was out of sight. She hated to admit to herself that this meant she was attracted to him, but there was no other way to explain it.

Since she had no apparent appeal for him, it shouldn't be a problem if she just remained calm over the next few days.

Calm. She'd always been calm. Then her private life had fallen apart, followed shortly by her professional life. Then she seemed to have lost her common sense.

But that was over. She was coming back. She just had to remember not to blow it all by responding with adolescent yearning to her kind but unwilling host.

She fell asleep, assuring herself that she had everything under control.

Chapter Five

"Ben, it's Mom."

Ben had a wrench on a pipe connector in the Bijou's basement in one hand, and his cell phone in the other.

"Hi, Mom. Everything okay?"

"I wanted you to know I've just come from your place and Natalie's fast asleep. I put the casserole in the fridge. Bake it at 350 for forty-five minutes."

"Got it. Thanks, Mom."

"You need me to pick up the girls?"

"No, I'll be finished soon. You're a peach. I owe you big."

"Try to remember that."

"I'm sure you'll remind me if I forget."

"Ben?"

"Yeah?"

"She seems like a lovely young woman."

"Yes, she does."

"She likes the girls."

"The girls are very likable."

"I think you should—you know—get to know her."

Ben had known where this conversation was leading. He got his own persistence from his mother.

"It'll be hard to avoid that with her living under my nose," he said, working the wrench with one hand.

His mother sighed. "Bentley, you know what I mean."

"Yes, I do, Mom. But it's not going to happen."

"I know you're not afraid of being hurt again. You don't have a cowardly bone in your body."

He had to put the wrench down and concentrate on his busybody mother. "I'm not afraid of being hurt, but I know I'll never find someone who'll love me and the girls like Julie did. I'd rather be alone than try to be happy with anyone else. And I think it'd be better for the girls."

"Julie was rare and special. But I think Natalie is, too. You attract special women."

"I didn't attract her, Mom. You made me come and get her and put her up."

"You know," she said, her voice taking on an edge of impatience, "you keep blaming me for this, but what you're ignoring is the fact that while I *did* ask you to take her in, she could have been any one of thousands of ordinary women, but she isn't. She's a sweet, gentle girl who ended up in a mess because she was trying to do the right thing. And do you think her fall wasn't fate?"

"I left a two-by-four on the—"

"I know, but in all the years you've been doing your work, no one's ever been injured because of you."

"Mom…"

"I'm just saying that some things in life are important and you should pay attention to them."

He was beginning to lose his place in the argument. "Thank you, Mom. I've got to go if I'm going to be done in time to get the girls."

"Okay. I love you."

"You love to harass me."

"Of course. That's one of the perks of motherhood."

The water heater was finally connected, but Ben had to retrace everything he'd done, afraid the distraction of his mother's call might have made him forget some important step or do it wrong.

Satisfied that the water heater was functional, he turned it on, then stayed around for a while to make sure it worked. It did.

He picked up Vanessa at school, then Roxie at the day care center.

Roxie climbed into the back of the car and Ben cinched her in place, reaching over to double-check Vanessa's seat belt.

He backed out of the car and found himself face to predatory grin with Marianne Beasley. She held a screaming two-year-old boy in her arms. His impatience with whatever the problem was had reached rage proportions. Roxie had gotten there several times at that age. He knew it well.

"Hi!" Marianne shouted at him over the noise. "Sorry about the racket! He was trying to eat the mums around the back porch! I'd like to talk to you about expanding the nap room and adding bunks!"

He smiled regretfully, knowing with whom she wanted to nap. "I'm sorry, I'm swamped at the moment. I wouldn't be able to get to it for months."

"That'd be okay! Can you come one day next week and give me an estimate?"

He couldn't think with the toddler screaming. "Sure. Okay," he replied.

"Monday? Tuesday?"

The best he could do was postpone it as long as possible. "How about Friday?"

"Friday's fine!"

He nodded amiably and walked around to the driver's side. She followed him, baby still screeching.

"You have a houseguest?" she asked, clearly waiting for an explanation.

He must have looked surprised, possibly even annoyed.

Her expression changed from her usual good cheer to watchful uncertainty. "Henrietta Caldwell is my ex-mother-in-law." She added candidly, but with a slightly nervous laugh, "She spies on you for me."

Even if he did ever consider dating again, he thought in grim amazement, he doubted he'd have the aptitude for it.

"She's doing a good job," he said with barely restrained impatience as he opened his door. "I do have a guest." And he perversely left it at that. "See you tomorrow, Marianne."

"Bye, Ben," she said, a worried frown now in place as she took a step backward so he could pull away. The toddler had her hair in both hands and was pulling as he screamed.

"How'd your day go, Rox?" Ben asked into the rearview mirror as he turned toward home.

Roxie held up a paper turkey, which was, curiously, colored lavender and chartreuse. Her handprint was evident in the design, the fingers becoming feathers. "It's a gobbler!" she said, and delivered several high-pitched gobble-gobbles.

"Turkeys are brown," Vanessa informed her.

Facts never concerned Roxie. "Mine's purple and green."

"But real ones are brown."

"Not mine."

Vanessa, who loved facts, groaned from behind him. "Daddy."

"Maybe it's a Martian turkey," he suggested.

"Nobody's been to Mars yet," she corrected him. "Just a robot thing."

He nodded. "But that doesn't mean the turkeys aren't there. Just because the robot didn't see any."

"That's silly." She sounded disdainful.

"Sometimes you have to be silly," he replied. He sometimes worried about how seriously she looked at everything. He tried to remember if she'd been that way before Julie's death, but couldn't recall. He'd been very involved in their upbringing, but Julie had been an in-charge kind of mother who never lost a detail of the children's care, so he'd trusted her to be on top of such things. "You should try it."

"Mom was never silly."

"Mom was silly all the time," he corrected with a laugh. "Just usually after you'd gone to bed. She thought everybody should have a lot of fun. We did a lot of fun things, remember?"

"I remember," Vanessa confirmed, "but she took really good care of us. And you can't do that if you're silly."

"You can't do it at the same time, maybe, but you can be silly when you don't have to be responsible and serious."

She didn't answer.

"Is the lady gone?" Roxie asked.

"No, she isn't. She fell down and hurt her leg, so she's going to stay with us for a couple of days."

There was wild excitement in the back seat. Apparently being delighted was more acceptable than being silly.

If Natalie had been asleep when they arrived home, she wasn't when the girls burst through the door and assailed the sofa.

"Hi!" Natalie said a little sleepily as she sat up to greet the girls. "I hope I'm not taking anybody's place. Do you usually sit here to do your homework, Vanessa?"

Vanessa shook her head. "I do it in my room. And Roxie's too little to have any."

"I'm not little!" Roxie returned crossly. "I'm just not very big yet."

Natalie defused the argument by noticing the artwork in Roxie's hand. "Look at that!" she said, studying it carefully. "What a great turkey."

"It's green and purple!" Roxie pointed out the obvious.

"I see that." Natalie said seriously. "It must be a turkey from another planet."

"That's what Daddy said," Vanessa noted, clearly impressed. "He thinks it's from Mars, even though the robot didn't see any."

"Could be," Natalie agreed. "What did you do today, Vanessa?"

"Just math and English," Vanessa answered, "and we cut out pumpkins and turkeys for the windows." She cast a slightly disparaging glance at her little sister. "American turkeys," she clarified. "What did you do? Daddy says you fell and hurt your leg."

"I slept a lot," Natalie said, "so my leg will get better quickly."

"I'm glad you can't go home," Vanessa admitted in a rush, then added, "I'm sorry you got hurt, but I'm glad you're still here."

"Yeah," Roxie affirmed.

The girls settled onto the sofa, one on each side of Natalie.

"Natalie would probably like to rest a little more before dinner," Ben said, a bit concerned about the deepening rapport between her and the girls. His daughters would be very disappointed when she left in a few days.

Natalie smiled up at him, looking rested and renewed by the girls' interest. "If it's all right with you, they're fine here."

Was it all right with him? He wasn't sure. She probably was justified in hiding out in a B-and-B and trying to forget the public ridicule and all the unhappiness of her situation.

But she was still a television personality with a tendency toward trouble, and she was going to be out of their lives in a matter of days.

Vanessa and Roxie, though, were so thrilled with her presence that it was hard for him to rain on their parade.

"All right," he conceded. "But if you get tired, or you just need some space, please tell them and they'll cooperate." He looked from one girl to the other and they nodded eagerly.

"Okay," he said. "I'll be in the office. Grandma brought us a casserole, so dinner will be in about an hour and a half."

"I'll set the table," Vanessa promised.

Ben retreated to his room at the back of the house, feeling a sudden disturbing sense of femininity in the house. He couldn't explain it; Natalie was barely able to move, but she seemed to be having an effect on the atmosphere.

There was the scent of gardenias in the air and a certain excitement that hadn't been present in some time. Even behind his desk some distance from the kitchen he could hear chatter and giggles and Roxie's high-pitched squeal. And then a burst of female laughter.

He experienced a pang right in the middle of his heart. He used to hear that sound when Julie was alive and she and the girls were baking or playing at something. It was very feminine and gave him a curious sense of well-being.

But it didn't do that for him today. Today it worried him. Because he liked the sound of it.

NATALIE HEARD the telephone, then the deep, calm
sound of Ben's voice answering it. She glanced at the
clock and decided that, if he did intend dinner for the
time he'd said, he was going to need help.

She struggled up onto her crutches as she'd done
several times during the day to visit the bathroom or
pour a cup of coffee. Then she asked Roxie to open
the refrigerator for her so that they could put the casserole into the oven.

"Vanessa, do you know how to set the table?"

"Yes, I do. Knives and spoons on the right, and
forks on the left."

"Okay. You do that. Sounds like your father got a
phone call, so let's surprise him by getting things
ready."

She put on a light to dispel the early evening
gloom, and the girls bustled while she hobbled about
the kitchen. Leaning on her crutches, she made a fresh
pot of coffee. She found Parmesan cheese to go with
the spaghetti casserole and asked Vanessa to bring the
salad makings to the counter so that she could wash
and prepare them.

When Ben rushed into the kitchen fifteen minutes
later, apologizing that dinner would be late, the girls
giggled at his surprise.

"We're making dinner 'cause you were on the
phone," Vanessa said. "Natalie can move around really good on her crutches. She made coffee and salad
and everything!"

Ben looked pleased. "Thank you," he said as the
girls went into his arms. "You're sure that's good for
your leg?"

It was beginning to throb a little, but she'd taken a pill and was sure she'd survive. Was he concerned that if she further injured herself she'd have to stay longer? She decided that she couldn't continue to second-guess everything he said.

"I feel fine," she said. "It's a little sore, but I guess it's going to be before it heals. Did you have anything particular in mind for dessert?"

"We have ice cream and cookies," Vanessa said.

"Perfect." Natalie checked the timer on the oven. "You still have twenty-two minutes," she said to Ben, "if there's anything else you have to do before dinner."

He held up his hands. "Just wash my hands and…anticipate."

Lulu's casserole was delicious. Conversation centered around Vanessa's need to collect fall leaves for a class project and Roxie's ability to recite the alphabet and count to 100.

Natalie made the mistake of expressing interest, and they were immediately treated to a recitation of both.

Ben distracted Roxie from a second round of the alphabet with compliments on her turkey drawing, now attached to the refrigerator with a magnet.

"We're going to have a *real* turkey," Roxie told Natalie, "when we go to Grandma's for Thanksgiving."

"Will you still be here?" Vanessa asked.

Natalie shook her head. "I should be all healed in the next couple of days. But having turkey at your grandma's sounds wonderful. I'm sorry I'll miss it."

"Do you have a grandma that cooks turkey?" Roxie leaned toward her inquisitively with a full milk mustache.

Natalie shook her head. Holidays were always a trial for her, but she knew many people had similar situations with their families, and tried to remember to be grateful that she had one.

"My mom usually has a big dinner catered," Natalie said.

Both girls frowned.

"Catering," Ben explained, "is when you hire a fancy restaurant, or someone whose job it is to cook for other people, to bring and serve the food."

Vanessa looked concerned. "Do you have leftovers?"

"Sometimes. A little bit."

"We get a whole pumpkin pie to bring home!" Vanessa said, her eyes wide at the prospect of the same windfall this year. "And lots of turkey and dressing and sweet potatoes."

"And Jell-O!" Roxie added, poking Vanessa in the arm lest she forget that important detail.

"Oh, yeah!" Vanessa leaned forward eagerly. "Grandma makes this red Jell-O with peaches and cherries in it and there's cottage cheese on the bottom and whipped cream on the top."

"That sounds wonderful." Natalie could imagine the four of them gathered around Lulu's table, which would be laden with all their favorite dishes. "My favorite thing is the dressing. What does your grandma put in hers?"

The girls turned to Ben.

"Sausage and apples," he said. "It's out of this world." He studied Natalie in mild concern. "Maybe we should overnight you a care package. A catered Thanksgiving dinner, while certainly better than none, sounds…"

"Awful?" she asked with a wistful smile. "It's not really that bad, it's just that nothing has those special touches that family recipes have. And we don't have sandwiches at night, or a wishbone to dry and wish on. But you can't have everything."

His concern turned to smiling sympathy. "Thanksgiving leftovers should be an inalienable right."

She shrugged. "Sometimes you just can't do anything about the way things are. I tried to turn my life around and succeeded only in messing everything up beyond repair."

"Nothing is ever beyond repair," he insisted. "You just have to sit back and try to look outside the box." He rolled his eyes. "I hate trendy expressions, but that one's apt, particularly here. There's a solution to your family issues somewhere. You just have to put yourself outside the boundaries you've given the problem and you'll get a different, creative perspective."

She'd thought the sperm bank was a creative solution to her problem of loneliness, but she didn't want to bring that up in front of the girls. So she remained silent.

Ben served dessert, strawberry-white chocolate ice cream with chocolate chip cookies.

"This reminds me of our pig-out parties in the dorm in college," Natalie said, dipping her cookie into the ice cream. "We'd all bring whatever we had to someone's room and eat while we studied."

Ben grinned. "You studied. That's a step up from my college dorm. We ate and watched wrestling. You haven't had ice cream and cookies for dessert since college?"

She shook her head. "I have to eat very carefully and stay in shape because every extra pound is highlighted by the television camera. I jog and go to the gym and almost never have anything with sugar in it."

"Are you happy with your life?" he asked. There was genuine interest in his eyes. "I mean, apart from the family issues."

Happy. Was she happy? It had been a long time since there'd been an opportunity to worry about happiness. Since she'd gotten the KRTV spot, she'd done everything to perfect her skills as a reporter and as a television personality, and to improve the physical image viewers saw on their screens.

She'd made good friends on the job, but there'd been little time for friends outside of work. And she'd had only that one disappointing attempt at romance.

The truth was, she was driven and lonely.

"Happy," she answered finally, "is an awful lot to ask for in this world."

He nodded as though he agreed with that assessment. "But you do have the right to ask for it," he added.

She studied him across the table. "Have you asked for it?"

He sighed. "I've had it."

"And…you're just going to let it be over?"

Touché! he thought with a grin. "Sometimes you just can't do anything about the way things are."

Dessert finished, Ben insisted that Natalie go back to the sofa while he and the girls cleared the table. Afterward, Vanessa went to do her homework.

"Want me to move you onto the living room sofa so you can watch television?" Ben asked Natalie. "I'm going to take Roxie upstairs for her bath."

"Thanks, but I'll be fine here." She lay back wearily against her pillows. "I took another pill just before dinner and I'm feeling tired. But please don't let that stop you from doing whatever you have to do. I think if you had to wax and buff the kitchen floor I could sleep through it."

"All right. I'll be down in a little bit. If you need anything, holler. I'm sure Vanessa will hear you if I don't."

Natalie lay in the shadowy kitchen and tried to take Ben's advice.

What outside-of-the-box angle was there to having a baby that she hadn't already considered?

There was adoption, but she worried about passing inspection as a potential parent. She could provide well for a baby, but she spent many hours on the job. Though she felt sure she could work out that problem with a little help from the station and a nanny, she wondered how an adoption agency would feel about it.

Considering how her efforts at the fertility clinic had failed, though, that might be the only option left.

Unless Ben was right, and it was the clinic experience that had been wrong.

Her heart kicked against her ribs as her brain formed a thought that had lingered there undefined for the past several hours. Ben would be the perfect candidate to father her baby. His children were beautiful and smart. Not simply because he'd fathered them, but because he was raising them.

She wouldn't ask that, of course. All she wanted was impregnation; he needn't provide anything else.

She'd known him only a day, but she knew him to be kind and caring. She would be safe in entering into such a bargain with him, and her baby would undoubtedly be blessed with his good qualities.

But she didn't have the courage to ask him. She hadn't made the best first impression on him, and she had nothing to offer him in return.

Still, he'd been the one who'd just told her she had the right to ask for happiness. All he could say was no.

It was another two days before she had the nerve to broach the subject.

BEN FOUGHT a recalcitrant bathroom sink drain on the Bijou's second floor most of the day on Wednesday. Once he'd thought he had the problem beaten, but it simply reappeared downstairs.

He'd called the school to have Vanessa transported to the day care on the Traveling Tots bus, then called Marianne to tell her Vanessa was coming and that he'd be later than usual picking up the girls.

"Shall I fix something for dinner?" she asked hopefully.

"Thanks, but my mother's taken care of it," he fibbed. Well, technically she had. He had a chicken and penne pasta casserole in the freezer, leftovers from dinner at her place two weeks ago.

"Your loss," Marianne teased. "I make a mean goulash."

"I'm sure you do. Roxie's always raving about your food."

As she absorbed the compliment, he took the opportunity to say goodbye.

It was just after five when he was satisfied that the drains on all floors ran free. He was pleased that he'd solved the problem, but was feeling crotchety anyway.

He put a Nat King Cole disc in the CD player in the van in an attempt to alter his mood before he picked up the girls.

Natalie was responsible for his mood. He hated to admit it, but it was true. She'd hobbled around for a couple of days, doing her best to help out, to repay him for providing nothing more than a place to stay and three meals a day. Except for the occasional cough, she was over her cold.

The sofa was now the girls' afternoon hangout. Vanessa poured milk, Roxie got the cookie tin and the three of them sat together discussing the day. Topics included Justin Blake, who was suddenly the bane of Vanessa's existence at school, and Roxie's new discovery that putting letters of the alphabet together made sounds.

Ben was pleased that the girls were having such a good time, yet selfishly felt left out, even replaced.

He'd noticed yesterday that Natalie was moving a little more freely, and this morning he'd even seen her without the crutches. She'd be going soon.

Well, that was good because he didn't need this aggravation. He didn't need to care like this.

She was nothing like Julie had been. She made outrageous choices to solve the problems in her life, and she was a television personality, for God's sake. It was Philadelphia and not L.A., but still a solid market. Her financial picture was probably a lot brighter than his.

He had his future planned. Hard work to feed the girls' college funds and fill his lonely hours. And someday, when the girls finally did build lives of their own, he might travel.

A walking tour of Europe had always appealed to him, and he'd still be young enough to enjoy it. It would be liberating to travel according to his own schedule, to see what he wanted to see, and stay as long as he chose or move on as the spirit moved him.

He stopped at a light as Cole's velvet voice sang that if he fell in love, it would be forever. Ben understood that. It had happened to him, and death didn't break the bond.

He was crazy to worry about this, he told himself as he watched the east-west traffic move across the intersection. He probably held no appeal for Natalie Browning anyway, so there was little point in arguing himself out of finding her appealing. She'd made it clear that she had no need for a man in her life, so there was no problem.

He'd simply gotten used to having her around, that was all. She smelled of gardenias all the time, she made the girls laugh and she was always trying to help.

He was cranky, he admitted to himself grimly as the light turned green and he accelerated, because he was going to miss her.

Luck was with him. He managed to dodge Marianne, who was occupied with another parent across the lawn and could only wave when he picked up the girls. Both were in a good mood. When he opened the back door of the house, he couldn't believe the aroma that greeted his exploratory sniff.

"Spareribs and sauerkraut?" he asked Natalie in disbelief. She sat at the table, spreading white icing on a chocolate cake.

She smiled up at him as the girls ran to dip index fingers in the pan of icing. "Your mother calls me twice a day to make sure I'm all right, and she mentioned once that it was your favorite meal."

"But where did you get the ingredients?"

"Coast Groceries delivers," she replied, apparently surprised he didn't know that. Then she nudged Vanessa toward the counter. "Get that bottle of sprinkles, sweetie, and you and Roxie can put them on the cake."

He pointed to a hollowed out pumpkin in the middle of the table. "Did they also deliver that?"

"The pumpkin, yes," she replied. "The fall leaves I picked up in the backyard."

He went closer to examine them. "But they're dried."

"Yeah. I did that in the microwave." She turned her attention to helping Vanessa sprinkle little chocolate things over half the cake, then gave the bottle to Roxie. That done, she focused on him again. "I wanted to pay you back for your hospitality."

"Thank you," he said, touched and alarmed at the same time. "I'd say it wasn't necessary, but I can't wait to taste it."

"Seventeen minutes," she said, glancing up at the clock.

"She made a chocolate cake, Daddy!" Roxie exclaimed. "With sprinkles!" She held up the small plastic bottle.

"Aren't we lucky?" he asked. "Go wash your hands so we don't hold up dinner when it's ready."

The girls scampered off.

Natalie looked up at him, her expression one of attempted innocence, but something about the look in her eyes hit him with the power of a body blow. He felt it deep inside and for a long time, though she looked away hurriedly and busied herself with touching up the rim of the cake.

Wondering what that look meant, he headed to the bathroom off his office to wash his own hands. Was she experiencing some of the same things he felt? Did he have some appeal for her he hadn't noticed before? Or was it indeed just gratitude?

He didn't know whether to be flattered or worried. He found out after he put the girls to bed.

He went back to the kitchen, intent on having another cup of coffee and a second piece of cake, and noticed that the sofa was empty. As was the kitchen and the living room.

The front door was partially open and he went to investigate. Natalie stood on the porch, hugging herself.

The air was cold and filled with the smell of pine and salt and wood smoke.

"You want a jacket?" he asked.

She shook her head. "Thanks. I'm about to come in. I was just feeling a little cabin fever, and the air here is so amazing. It's like something you should pay one hundred dollars an ounce for."

He laughed lightly and leaned in the open doorway. "If you have rain eight months out of the year, it keeps the people away. And that keeps the air clean."

She sighed, something clearly on her mind. "I love it here. It would never keep me away. Living in a crowded big city makes you realize that sunshine isn't everything."

"Literally?" he asked. "Or figuratively?"

She hooked an arm around the column that supported the porch, leaned out over the dark lawn and looked at the light-spangled view of downtown Dancer's Beach below them. "Both, I guess. I've certainly had enough stormy times in my life during the past few months to make me realize that pain and humiliation aren't fatal."

"That's the spirit," he cheered gently. "Don't let them stop you. Go back home and find another brilliant story, and look for a stronger, more worthy man to love than what's-his-name turned out to be."

She turned away from the sequined view with what appeared to be sudden purpose. She looked nervous but determined.

"I will find another good story," she said, looking into his eyes. "But I'm going to stay on my course of finding a baby to love rather than a man."

He closed his eyes, wondering why in God's name she insisted on doing this. "Natalie," he groaned. "Have you learned nothing from this experience? Not that *I'm* anyone you should listen to, but it's—"

"On the contrary," she interrupted in a firm tone. "I've listened. You were right. The sterile clinic atmosphere scared me. I should try to make a baby the more conventional way."

"But you just said you wanted to find a baby rather than a man."

"I know." She looked him in the eye, and he felt that jolt again. "Ben?" she asked, her voice high but steady, "would you father my baby?"

Chapter Six

He had excellent hearing. He had neither misunderstood nor misinterpreted that…request. But he could only stare at her for a moment, at a complete loss for words.

She hurried to explain, as though that would somehow clarify things for him.

"I promise you that's absolutely all I want from you. I know you have this wonderful life going with the girls and your mother and your work, and I swear I don't want to intrude on that in any way. Nor do I want any kind of support—emotional or financial." She paused to draw a breath, something desperate in her eyes. In the darkness of the front porch, she was almost like a figment of his imagination, a beautiful, porcelain face blooming out of the night. "It's just that your children are so wonderful, and I know that's because they're half you. And maybe if I wasn't—you know—in a lab situation I…I could do it."

She was now shivering uncontrollably. He guessed that was as much the result of the difficult subject as the cold wind picking up, but he caught her arm and drew her inside.

She hobbled in, her expression grim. "You think I'm insane ," she guessed.

He sat her in a big, comfortable chair by the fireplace, propping her leg on a matching ottoman. "I think you have insane ideas," he replied, sitting beside her feet. "Natalie, you don't even know me."

"I know you're a good, kind man," she replied. "Women marry men they don't know as well as I think I know you. I've seen you in action with your girls and your mother, and that tells me a lot."

He was flattered by her apparent conviction that *good* and *kind* did describe him. But there was a lot more to him—some of it good, but some of it less admirable.

Like the inclination to give her what she wanted and hang the consequences, simply because he hadn't made love with a woman since Julie, and he'd been watching Natalie's seductive little caboose bobble around his kitchen for several days now. Lust was stirring inside him.

She studied his face and sighed with reluctant acceptance. "You're not buying this, are you?"

He was an idiot, but in light of her opinion of him, he had to be a good idiot. "I'm afraid not," he said gently, giving her feet a pat. "I couldn't father a child and just walk away. I *am* a father. I know what it takes out of you every day to provide a child with what it needs to grow physically and emotionally. And I know what it gives you back. I couldn't do that and not be part of its life."

He saw a flicker of hope in her eyes. He didn't understand what he'd done wrong until she said eagerly, "Lots of women are raising children with the help of fathers who don't live with them, and they still manage to be families. If you—"

"No," he said firmly. "Everyone has to do what works for them. But I couldn't be a long-distance parent, or a Saturday parent. I understand that many fathers have no choice, but I do. No child of mine is going to live across the country from me and see me only occasionally."

She nodded, disappointment in her eyes, but gracious acceptance in her smile. "I understand, of course. I hope I haven't upset or embarrassed you."

"Hardly." He grinned. "Having a beautiful woman invite me to make love to her is one of my favorite fantasies. If there wasn't the possibility of so many repercussions, you'd get an entirely different answer."

"Thank you," she whispered.

"Want to watch *Lake Placid?*" he asked, eager to take the sting out of his rejection. As though a giant crocodile would do it, but it would be a distraction that she'd enjoy. "I'll make popcorn."

She sat up. "Sounds like a plan. Can I keep this chair?"

"You bet. Hold on. I'll put the popcorn in the microwave and find the film."

You are insane, Ben told himself hours later. They'd enjoyed the movie. Then he'd carried Natalie upstairs to her room and gone to bed himself. The long-dormant lust within him had stirred at the possibility of relief, and now stomped around inside, apparently annoyed at being denied.

Ben stared at the ceiling until sometime after three, then finally fell asleep out of sheer exhaustion.

He awoke to the aroma of breakfast cooking and sat up abruptly to look at the clock. It lay on its side. Did he have a vague memory of being awakened by it and slapping it into silence?

He righted it now and read the time with a groan: 8:08. Vanessa would be late for school!

Without taking the time to shower, he pulled on his clothes and hurried to the girls' rooms. They were both empty.

He turned to head down the hall and found Natalie blocking his path. She was wearing the brown turtleneck and cords she'd worn the morning she'd intended to fly back home. A white tea towel was tied around her waist.

"Good morning," she said amiably. "Don't worry about the girls. I took them to school."

He put a hand to his foggy eyes. "You...drove my van?"

She laughed lightly. "Yes, and it's still in one piece. Vanessa gave me perfect directions to the school, then told me to 'stay straight for another eleven blocks to get to the day care center.' She was right, too. It's exactly eleven blocks. I made the girls pancakes for breakfast and there's enough batter left to make you a few. If I add a couple of pieces of bacon and an egg, would that see you through to your coffee break?"

Pancakes? Bacon and an egg?

He dropped his hands to his hips and focused on her lightly but perfectly made-up face and the fluffy golden hair curled on her forehead and around her ears. She didn't look at all like a woman who'd had her dreams of motherhood shattered last night.

"You're awfully perky," he said, mildly accusing. "You must have slept better than I did."

She nodded, her smile philosophical. "There's something to be said for knowing what your options are, even when you're down to one."

"One?" he asked. "You have another prospect to father your child?"

"No. I think I'll try to adopt. My work schedule might put an agency off, but it's worth a try. So...yes on the pancakes?"

"Yes," he said. "Ten minutes?"

"Perfect." She bustled off in the direction of the stairs.

He spent nine minutes standing under a hot shower, then one minute getting dressed.

He hurried through the kitchen as she put pancakes on a plate. "I'll be back in a second," he promised. "I just remembered that I left my wallet and my keys in the office last night."

"I'll just keep it warm in the oven," she said. "Take your time."

The woman was too amenable to be real, he thought as he walked into the office and went to the desk. He found the keys immediately, but had to rummage under blueprints and plans for his wallet.

The phone rang and he hit the speaker button. He opened his mouth to say "Hello," but the greeting came out in a higher, feminine voice. Natalie had picked up the kitchen phone.

"Natty!" a woman's deep voice said angrily.

"Mom?" Natalie asked in surprise.

Ben was just about to hit the end button to give them privacy when the deep voice said with recrimination, "You are all over the news this morning! It seems Chana Brown, the actress, used the same sperm bank you did and is now suing for ten million dollars because she *is* pregnant. So, of course, it brought up everything about you again. *And* it said that *The Snitch* reports this morning that you were seen in Dancer's Beach in the company of a 'local entrepreneur.'" She stressed the last two words as though they were a quote. "I've tried to find one on the stands, but they're apparently sold out. The picture they showed on the news was of you being carried and put in a van by this man!"

"Mom, I'm—"

"I called all over creation to find you. Your office said you went to see your cousin, but Dori doesn't answer, so I called the Buckley Arms, but you weren't registered. They told me the only other inn in town was a B-and-B. So I called there and the owner told me how to find you. Natalie, how could you do this to your family? This is just another nail in my coffin, Natty. Another nail."

"I was hurt and Ben helped me," Natalie said hurriedly, forcefully. "That's all it was! And thank you for trusting everyone else's report of what happened but mine!"

"I couldn't trust yours because I couldn't find you to ask you!"

"You just found me and you didn't ask, you accused!"

"What are you doing at his home?" her mother asked stiffly.

"He offered his hospitality because the room I used at his mother's B-and-B was booked for this week."

"Well, you're a celebrity. You should exercise a little discretion."

There was the smallest pause. Ben wondered if Natalie was remembering her brandy and cold medication experience and thinking her mother might be right.

He hated the thought that Natalie should be persecuted for what had been an unwise but understandable reaction to a very bad situation—and by her own mother. In the same situation, his mother would have told him he'd been thoughtless, then gone out and tracked down whoever had maligned him and made them pay.

"Mother, Ben Griffin is the kindest, dearest man I've ever known, with two of the sweetest little girls in the whole world. Nothing has happened that requires discretion. I apologize if you're embarrassed, but maybe you should be less concerned with how things look and what people think and more interested in what's really happening. Goodbye, Mother."

There was a loud slam and the line was disconnected.

Ben sat in the chair at his desk and closed his eyes, fighting the impulse that was building inside him. No.

No. It would be stupid. It might help her, but it would do nothing but complicate his already difficult life.

And what was his *real* motive? To help her, or to help himself?

He gave that a moment's thought and couldn't decide. He picked up his wallet and keys and went into the kitchen.

"Found them," he said, holding them up as he went toward her. "Anything I can do to help?"

She smiled, pretending good humor, but he could see the distress in her eyes. She hardly limped now, he noticed absently. "No, thanks. Everything's ready." She brought two plates to the table, then went back to the counter to pour two cups of coffee.

She sat opposite him, looking fresh and beautiful despite her mother's harangue. "I want to thank you for letting me stay here," she said politely. "I'd have probably had to stay on a park bench if you hadn't. But after breakfast, I really should be on my way."

"You're going back to Philadelphia?" he asked cautiously, spreading butter on his pancakes. They were light and crepelike.

"I may just travel around awhile," she replied, peppering her eggs, then handing him the pepper mill. "Maybe drive down the coast. Dori's always telling me how dramatic it is this time of year."

The words were on the tip of his tongue. Oddly, everything inside him seemed to accelerate as he opened his mouth to speak them. His heart was beating hard. Many times over the past eighteen months he'd felt as though it had stopped altogether.

"Would you like company on this trip?" he asked, phrasing the question lightly so that it didn't terrify her—or him.

Her gaze flew to his as she tried to read his meaning. *"Company."* She repeated the word uncertainly.

He had to speak more plainly or he wouldn't be sure what he was talking about, either.

"Coast-exploring, baby-making company," he said clearly.

He saw the happiness explode in her eyes, but it lasted only a moment. Then suspicion and concern appeared there.

"Why?"

"Change of heart," he said.

Natalie's eyes bored into his. His mother could do that same thing. Roxie, too. "Did you overhear my conversation with my mother?" she demanded.

He considered lying, but those eyes wouldn't allow it. "Every word," he said, explaining about hitting the speaker button when the phone rang as he searched for his keys.

Her eyes cooled further and her jaw firmed. "So this is a pity concession."

He gave her the same look in return. "Not at all. I've been thinking it over and decided that I can fulfill your request, after all, if I'm allowed a few stipulations of my own."

Her eyes softened slightly as she put her fork down. "And those are?"

"That you agree to stay until we know whether or not you're pregnant. And if you are, that you agree to stay until the baby's born, and then we decide how

I can be involved in the baby's life, and we insure those agreements legally.''

No, NO, NO! Natalie thought. If she agreed to those terms, she would lose control of a situation she wanted to be entirely hers, of the baby who would be the receptacle of all the love she had to give that no one else seemed to want.

But if she refused, she would lose the opportunity to have a baby. And, in a flash of insight, she saw ahead to the lives of two little children—one with an anonymous sperm-donor father, and the other with a father who was active and involved in his life.

"Okay," she heard herself say in some surprise. "But, you're sure?"

"I'm sure. Are you?"

She was. She'd worry about those details later, but she wanted a baby desperately. And now that she knew Ben, she wanted *his* baby, specifically. "I'm sure."

He offered his hand across the table and she took it.

The bargain sealed, he went back to his breakfast. "I'll ask Mom if she'll watch the girls for a couple of days. How long a trip did you have in mind?"

She was ovulating. She'd been watching her cycle for so long that she swore she could feel the physical difference.

"Four, five days? But…if you'd rather stay here, I'd—"

He shook his head. "I think the trip's a good idea. Neutral territory might make you more comfortable."

"Okay. But your mom is busiest in the morning, when the girls have to be taken to school and day care."

"Not a problem. There are a couple of mothers we've pooled with on occasion who are on the same routine. I'll promise them a week's driving in December if they'll pick up the girls from Mom's for a few days now."

"Well," Natalie said, feeling strangely breathless and just a little dizzy. This had all happened so suddenly, so unexpectedly. "I guess that's settled."

"At least until you're pregnant and we have to settle other things."

"Provided I *do* conceive."

"No reason to think you won't," he said. "Your doctor said you're fine, and I have two children, so we should be able to make another."

"Yeah," she said a little weakly. "I hope so."

"Don't worry," he assured her. "Things work best if you're relaxed about it."

She frowned at him, perplexed by his attitude. "You seem to have a sudden...enthusiasm for a project you swore you'd never undertake."

"That's true," he admitted. "Frankly, I don't know if this is wise or not, I just know that it always pays off to give a decision my wholehearted effort. It seems to make it work out, even if the plan was ill-advised in the first place."

"You realize," she stated frankly, feeling obliged to point this out, "that I have nothing to give you in return."

He raised an eyebrow in amused surprise. "You're not serious," he said.

What did that mean? "I don't understand," she admitted.

"Natalie," he scolded gently. "You aren't that much of an innocent, are you? I have the opportunity to make love to you. Repeatedly."

She was momentarily astonished that he considered that a sort of reward. Kyle had never considered it more than a temporary pleasure that didn't seem to have as much to do with her as with *it*.

Ben was further surprised by her puzzled face. "Come on, Nat. No man's ever been delighted by your charms?"

She shook her head, still surprised. "Well, there was only Kyle. And...no. Not delighted, simply... satisfied."

Ben looked at her for a long moment, and she saw something in the back of his eyes that brought the color to her cheeks. "You don't have to..." She waved her hand to express the thought she couldn't quite find the words for. "I mean, we just need the— you know—the clinical... You know."

"Sex should never be clinical," he said seriously. "Particularly sex to make a baby. No. We're not doing this like something that could be written up in a textbook. We're going for memories."

Memories. Longings that couldn't be satisfied when she returned to Philadelphia? "Is that wise?" she asked.

"Is any of this wise?" he returned.

She didn't know. He was causing her to have reservations. But he was also causing her an excitement she'd seen in other women but had never known herself. She felt a flash of the desire she'd once seen in Dori's eyes when she was looking at her husband.

"What if you regret it?" she asked.

"I won't," he said with a conviction that only served to stir that unaccustomed desire.

"What if I have to spend nine months in your spare room?"

He laughed. "I can deal with it if you can."

"Dear God," she whispered, half in prayer, half in confounded disbelief, "I'm going to have a baby!"

Chapter Seven

"A trip where?" Lulu asked. She and Ben sat in the middle of her green-pink-and-white kitchen with its coordinating wallpaper, curtains, and tiled backsplash that she'd handpainted herself and he'd installed. They were eating Danish apple cake left over from breakfast.

"Down the coast," Ben replied. "Four or five days. I've already called Molly Burger, who'll pick up the girls for school and bring them back to you. No special events this week, so your schedule shouldn't be too disrupted."

Lulu looked at him as she stirred sugar into her tea. She hadn't asked the reason for the trip and he hadn't volunteered.

"Does this mean your social life is active again?" He'd known she wouldn't be able to avoid asking forever.

"No," he replied patiently, "it just means I'm taking a trip."

"With a beautiful young woman who wants a baby."

Lulu pulled something off the seat beside her and

placed it next to his plate. It was *The Snitch,* the tabloid Natalie's mother had mentioned on the phone. Half the page above the fold was a very grainy photo of him carrying Natalie to the van. It had apparently been taken the morning he'd driven her to the clinic.

His mother looked grim. "Henrietta Caldwell recognized her and sold it to them for a considerable sum. She's off my list, I can tell you."

The brief story that followed was a series of outrageous insinuations and speculations about "the darling of the nightly news" and the Dancer's Beach entrepreneur.

He folded it and handed it back. "I like being called an entrepreneur," he said. "Gives building maintenance class."

His mother made a face. "Do you know what you're doing?" she asked.

He chewed a bite of cake and swallowed. "Am I the one in-line skating down Beach Avenue at age sixty-three?"

"Broken bones heal," she said. "A broken heart's another matter."

"I thought you liked her."

"I do. But I don't want anything to happen that's going to increase your problems. I want you to be happy, not…"

"We're not getting married, Mom," he reminded her. "We're just taking a trip together."

"Down Lullabye Lane?" she asked pointedly.

He pushed away from the table. "I've got to get back to work. Is it okay about the girls?"

She stood, too. She was wearing the same expression she'd worn the day he joined the marines without telling her first.

"Of course it's okay. Just take care. I think she'd be perfect for you, but if she doesn't know that and you get her... I mean, does she want you for you, or for the baby?"

"Mom..." he warned.

"'Cause I'll tell you I told you so when the time comes. You know I will."

He kissed her cheek and hurried off.

The girls were less than pleased that he and Natalie were taking a trip without them until he explained that when they returned, Natalie would be staying awhile.

They jumped up and down in excitement, and he suggested they all go upstairs and help each other pack.

He removed all the lumber and tools from the back of the van, then went upstairs to pack a few things for himself. He heard Natalie and the girls in Roxie's room, debating the wisdom of taking a bathing suit to Grandma's.

"It's too cold to swim!" Vanessa pointed out reasonably.

Roxie apparently packed it anyway. "I like to wear it under my Pooh overalls."

"It's okay," Natalie placated Vanessa. "It's probably like wearing Victoria's Secret stuff under your everyday clothes. It makes you feel special."

"Do you have Victoria's Secret stuff?" Vanessa asked, awe audible in her voice. Ben had had no idea she even knew the name.

"A few things."

"Let me see!"

He peered out his door in time to watch unnoticed as a little parade crossed the hall.

He heard oohs and ahhs. "Purple!" Roxie said. Then "Leopard!" from Vanessa.

"But this is my favorite," Natalie said.

There were more oohs and ahhs, but no identification of what color or pattern it was—or even *what* precisely it was.

As he packed a roll-necked sweater, he entertained the lusty thought that he'd eventually find out for himself.

"IF WE'RE THINKING in terms of rest and relaxation," Ben said as he drove south on Highway 101, "does shopping at the outlet mall or visiting the Chinook Winds Casino in Lincoln City fit into that?"

Natalie sat beside him, her hands folded primly in her lap. A curious restraint had overtaken her the moment Ben pulled out of the driveway a short twenty minutes ago.

"Would *you* like to go shopping?" she asked in a carefully modulated voice intended to hide her nervousness.

He gave her a quick glance that suggested the ploy had failed. "I asked you first," he teased. "My life is filled with women. I have enough experience that I can follow you around and carry your packages without feeling suicidal."

"I appreciate the offer," she demurred, "but we can stop if there's time on the way home. Usually I love malls, but I was thinking more in terms of enjoying the natural beauty of the coast.'' She held up a spray of brochures. ''I love to gamble, also, but let's save that for the drive home, too. There's so much other stuff to see.''

''Okay. What's our first stop?''

She pulled a brochure out of the handful and deposited the others in the front pocket of her purse. ''How about Depoe Bay, just south of Lincoln City?''

''Okay. I think they whale watch there.''

She remembered reading something about whales, and searched the brochure until she found it. ''Here it is. It says Depoe Bay is 'Oregon's favorite place for watching the migration of Gray Whales. Each spring the city hosts the Celebration of the Whales with harbor and whale watching tours.' Too bad it isn't spring.'' She turned over the folder. ''Did you know the name comes from a Siletz Indian named Charles Depot, so named because he worked for the U.S. Army Depot?''

''No, I didn't.''

''I suppose the spelling was just corrupted over time.''

''Thank you,'' Ben said gravely. ''I was worried about why it was spelled differently.''

She detected sarcasm and swatted him with the brochure. ''I thought that was interesting.''

He laughed. ''It was. But you don't have to learn every fact about every town on the coast. Just try to relax and enjoy what you're seeing.''

''I'm a reporter,'' she reminded him. ''Facts are my business.''

"You're a reporter *on vacation,*" he emphasized. "And for as long as that lasts, fun should be more important than facts."

She chose not to explain that the facts were a diversion at the moment from her concerns about what would happen when they finally stopped driving tonight. They were in agreement about this and she knew she was safe with him—at least from physical harm. But something was brewing inside her that she didn't entirely understand.

"Hopefully there's a bakery there," Ben said, putting one hand to his flat stomach as the other guided the car. "I'll be ready for a coffee break. You're not going to watch a diet or anything, are you?"

She made a scornful sound. "Like the one I've watched while eating your mother's casseroles and desserts? No, I won't. This trip is about self-indulgence."

Realizing belatedly how that might have sounded to him in view of their purpose, she studied his profile to see if he'd taken offense.

"Don't worry about it," he said, without even turning to look at her. "I understand that you're indulging your wish to have a baby, not a man, and not me, specifically."

That was brutally put, but made the point.

And when she heard it, she wasn't sure she liked it.

THEY DID FIND A BAKERY in a row of quaint little shops. Natalie ate a cream cheese Danish and sipped a mocha while standing on the rocks and looking down at the small harbor. Ben had polished off a cinnamon roll and now sipped coffee while standing behind her and watching a Coast Guard boat make its way across the bay. A scenic old bridge with a central arch spanned the distance from one side to the other. The air was cold, the sky overcast and spitting rain.

Natalie had brought a down vest, which she wore over a sweatshirt, but as the cold wind whipped in from the ocean, she wished she'd thought to button it before she'd filled her hands with pastry and coffee.

"Would you hold this, please?" she asked Ben, extending her hand to offer him her paper-wrapped Danish, then changing her mind and trying to hand him the coffee instead. "The way you scarfed your cinnamon roll, I don't trust you."

"And rightly so," he said, putting his coffee down on the rock. "You need your vest snapped?"

"Please."

He started from the bottom, his knuckles grazing the fly of her jeans. Sensation shot up through her and ricocheted like a bullet in a tight spot. She stood still, afraid to breathe.

Fortunately, he seemed to notice nothing as he continued his work. He pulled up her collar and pressed the top snap in place.

He ran his eyes over her hair. "You should have a hat," he said.

"Why? Is my hair all messed up?"

"No, but it's damp." He reached both hands up to rub her earlobes with his thumbs and forefingers. "And your ears are almost purple."

Sensation again—this time streaking through the

upper part of her body, centering inexplicably in the tips of her breasts.

She pointed at him with her coffee cup. "You don't have a hat," she said, her voice husky.

"I'm used to working outside. You're an indoors hothouse flower."

"I am not. I jog every other morning, rain or shine."

"You should do it in a hat."

"I do, I just didn't bring one with me. I expected to sit inside with Dori and complain about my lot in life." She smiled in self-deprecation. "Pathetic, huh?"

"No, but second, certainly, to vacationing down the coast. Come on. Finish that roll so we can find you a hat."

They located a sporting goods store in the lineup of shops. Ben picked up a simple, dark blue wool watch cap.

Natalie rolled her eyes over its lack of style. "I'd like to hear a focus group's comments on this."

Ben took it from her and, stretching it with his hands, pulled it onto her head. Her bangs and the hair at the sides of her face sprang out below in a curly fringe.

His eyes went over her and she saw them soften and linger on the hair peeking out.

"Do I look ridiculous?" she asked, standing on tiptoe to peer in the mirror standing atop a nearby shelf.

"You look better than anyone has a right to look

in a watch cap." He caught her hand, grabbed a larger hat in exactly the same style and went to the counter.

When they were outside again, he surprised her by turning not toward the car but in the opposite direction.

"Where we going?" she asked.

"There are no whales about," he replied as they strode along a walk that bordered the ocean, "but while you were picking out your roll, the baker told me that you can still see a 'spout.'"

He pointed a small distance ahead of them to a point where people stood in a cluster, watching the water below.

"Water is forced through underground lava tubes when the tide's in, and the surf sometimes blows sixty feet into the air."

They stood with everyone else and waited as nothing happened. Finally there was a small spray, then a taller burst that splashed up to the railing, then finally there was a loud whoosh as water shot up like a geyser many feet high.

They stayed to watch it happen again, then went back to the car and headed south again.

The highway climbed over four hundred feet above sea level to Cape Foulweather.

"We don't have to consult the brochure," Natalie said, "to figure out how the cape got its name."

"Good point. Otter Rock, which is coming up, too, is pretty self-explanatory. Want to stop at Devil's Punch Bowl?"

"Sure." She'd seen that in her brochure. "More

turbulent water, I think, but because of underwater caves.''

The water did churn like something in a witch's cauldron. Foam spewed and dampened the hardy on-lookers.

Natalie tipped her head back and drew in a deep gulp of the cold, fresh air. It smelled of salt, fish, and the pines that were everywhere.

"You going into a swoon on me?'' Ben asked, pulling her slightly back from the edge.

"I'm just trying to breathe in this wonderful air.''

"You're going to hyperventilate. And possibly become an ice cube in the punch bowl if you lean any farther over. I'm glad you're getting into this, but I'd rather it didn't happen literally.''

She made a face at him as he led her back to the car. "Spoilsport.''

"I'd rather stop your fun than have to jump in after you.''

"I can swim.''

"In the Devil's Punch Bowl?''

She subsided in her seat and watched the rugged scenery go by. High, roughly hewn rocks seemed to hang on the cliff's edge, and others looked as though they had been flung out to sea in some prehistoric eruption. The water churned and the wind blew. The deciduous trees, their red and gold leaves snowing down on the highway, leaned into the wind, while the pines stood straight, their long-needled arms rippling gracefully. Seagulls flew, seeming to make little headway.

"Tell me about your father,'' Ben said, surprising

her out of her study of the seascape and its inhabitants.

He'd been gone so long, it was hard for her to remember him. "He was very gentle and easygoing," she said finally, remembering how comforting his embrace had been. "My mother rode roughshod over him like she does everyone, but he seemed to maintain his own little bubble of seclusion where he was happy."

"But shut off from you?" Ben asked.

Natalie turned to him in surprise. She'd known that about her father on some level, but she'd never let herself form the thought because it was somehow disloyal.

"I'm sure that wasn't what he intended," she replied, defending him. "How did you know that?"

"Because I found that tendency in myself when we first lost Julie." The road curved and Ben concentrated on it until it straightened out again. "If I turned off all memory, all sensory receptors, I could almost bear it. But then the kids couldn't reach me. So I just had to let it hurt."

"I guess that never occurred to my father. When he was available to us, he was wonderful—funny and smart and very generous. But when Mom got to be too much, I guess it was easier to retreat than to fight her."

Ben nodded at the road. "Your mother takes no prisoners."

"She loves us." Again, Natalie felt called upon to defend a parent. "She's just a little heavy-handed with it. She thinks her way is the only way for all of us.''

"Your husband's going to have a rough road."

She shook her head. "I don't think I'm getting married."

"Why not?" He darted a glance at her on the straight stretch.

"Dating's too much trouble," she said with a sigh, "and the time my work requires doesn't allow for bumping into someone and fostering a relationship."

"And your mother's not on you about *that?*"

"All the time, but I'm standing firm."

He laughed mirthlessly. "My mother's been trying to fix me up with women for the past six months."

Natalie giggled. "I've noticed. But Vanessa tells me that Roxie's day care teacher has a crush on you."

He groaned. "I'm evading her."

"Maybe you shouldn't."

"I'm not getting married, either."

"How come?" She turned in her seat to study his profile. "You're the quintessential husband and father. It would be a crime against womanhood if you remained single."

"Oh, hardly. There's a lot about me you don't know yet."

"You mean the tendency to boss, and generally have things your way?" she asked, all innocence.

"That wasn't nice," he scolded, unable to look away from the road as he navigated a series of hairpin turns with high rock on one side and a sheer drop on the other. "Particularly after just softening me up with praise."

She laughed, thinking she hadn't had this much fun talking with a man since college.

"And knowing what you want is a good quality," he argued.

"But making it happen your way when other people are involved," she countered mercilessly, "is just bossy."

"Well...I'm used to dealing with crews of tough, confident men who'd argue about everything if I didn't make it clear who was in charge."

"So you've mistaken me for someone in a hard hat?"

"With that head," he replied, "you don't need a hard hat. Find something on the radio, will you please?"

She leaned forward to turn on the power. "Can we stop in Newport?" she asked over the sudden blaring of sound. She turned the volume down.

"We'll have lunch in Newport," he said, "and find someplace to stay. There's a lot to see and do there." Then, as an afterthought, he added, "That all right with you?"

"Yes. Thank you for consulting me, even if you did leave it a little late."

"Grumble, grumble."

BEN HADN'T EXPECTED to have such a good time doing small things. They had lunch in a restaurant overlooking the water, then found a place to stay in a series of cottages on a bluff. They looked as though they'd been appointed by a decorator from the Hamptons.

PLAY HARLEQUIN'S

LUCKY HEARTS

GAME

AND YOU GET

- ◆ **FREE BOOKS!**
- ◆ **A FREE GIFT!**
- ◆ **YOURS TO KEEP!**

TURN THE PAGE AND DEAL YOURSELF IN...

Play **LUCKY HEARTS** for this...

exciting FREE gift!
This surprise mystery gift could be yours free

when you play **LUCKY HEARTS!**
...then continue your lucky streak with a sweetheart of a deal!

1. Play Lucky Hearts as instructed on the opposite page.

2. Send back this card and you'll receive 2 brand-new Harlequin American Romance® novels. These books have a cover price of $4.25 each in the U.S. and $4.99 each in Canada, but they are yours to keep absolutely free.

3. There's no catch! You're under no obligation to buy anything. We charge nothing— ZERO—for your first shipment. And you don't have to make any minimum number of purchases—not even one!

4. The fact is thousands of readers enjoy receiving their books by mail from the Harlequin Reader Service®. They enjoy the convenience of home delivery...they like getting the best new novels at discount prices, BEFORE they're available in stores...and they love their *Heart to Heart* subscriber newsletter featuring author news, horoscopes, recipes, book reviews and much more!

5. We hope that after receiving your free books you'll want to remain a subscriber. But the choice is yours—to continue or cancel, any time at all! So why not take us up on our invitation, with no risk of any kind. You'll be glad you did!

Visit us online at

www.eHarlequin.com

◆ **Exciting Harlequin® romance novels—FREE!**
◆ **Plus an exciting mystery gift—FREE!**
◆ **No cost! No obligation to buy!**

YES!

I have scratched off the silver card. Please send me the 2 FREE books and gift for which I qualify. I understand I am under no obligation to purchase any books, as explained on the back and on the opposite page.

With a coin, scratch off the silver card and check below to see what we have for you.

HARLEQUIN'S

LUCKY HEARTS GAME

354 HDL C6QF

154 HDL C6P5
(H-AR-OS-07/01)

| | | | | | | | | | | | | |

NAME   (PLEASE PRINT CLEARLY)

ADDRESS

APT.#   CITY

STATE/PROV.   ZIP/POSTAL CODE

Twenty-one gets you 2 free books, and a free mystery gift!

Twenty gets you 2 free books!

Nineteen gets you 1 free book!

Try Again!

Offer limited to one per household and not valid to current Harlequin American Romance® subscribers. All orders subject to approval.

▼ DETACH AND MAIL CARD TODAY! ▼

The Harlequin Reader Service®—Here's how it works:

Accepting your 2 free books and gift places you under no obligation to buy anything. You may keep the books and gift and return the shipping statement marked "cancel." If you do not cancel, about a month later we'll send you 4 additional novels and bill you just $3.57 each in the U.S., or $3.96 each in Canada, plus 25¢ shipping & handling per book and applicable taxes if any.* That's the complete price and — compared to cover prices of $4.25 each in the U.S. and $4.99 each in Canada — it's quite a bargain! You may cancel at any time, but if you choose to continue, every month we'll send you 4 more books, which you may either purchase at the discount price or return to us and cancel your subscription.

*Terms and prices subject to change without notice. Sales tax applicable in N.Y. Canadian residents will be charged applicable provincial taxes and GST.

If offer card is missing write to: Harlequin Reader Service, 3010 Walden Ave., P.O. Box 1867, Buffalo, NY 14240-1867

BUSINESS REPLY MAIL
FIRST-CLASS MAIL   PERMIT NO. 717   BUFFALO, NY

POSTAGE WILL BE PAID BY ADDRESSEE

HARLEQUIN READER SERVICE
3010 WALDEN AVE
PO BOX 1867
BUFFALO NY 14240-9952

NO POSTAGE
NECESSARY
IF MAILED
IN THE
UNITED STATES

Ben and Natalie spent the afternoon at the aquarium, then returned to the cottage. Natalie made a production of looking through her things for something to wear to dinner. She was fidgety and going to great lengths to hide the fact.

So he pretended not to notice as he reclined on the bed. "There's dancing at the restaurant right across the highway," he said, perusing a brochure from the top drawer of the fashionably beachy-looking dresser.

She turned away from the small closet with a groan. "But you don't like to dance."

"I never said that," he corrected. "I said dancing and liking horror movies didn't sound like compatible pursuits. I didn't want you to search forever for a man you wouldn't be able to find."

"And yet *you* like horror movies and dancing?"

"I do. I'm just not husband material." He was beginning to wish he hadn't started this line of conversation. Considering why they were here, discussing his unwillingness to commit to her beyond their purpose seemed suddenly shallow—even selfish.

She, mercifully, seemed to feel more charity. She turned back to the closet. "Well, fortunately for you, I'm not looking for a husband. I did bring a little black dress." She swept it out of the closet and held it in front of her to show him.

It was very simple, with a square neckline and what looked like a close fitting waist and a flared skirt.

"Very pretty," he said. "And I brought a suit. Shall I make reservations?"

"You're sure you want to go dancing?"

It would be a good excuse, he thought, to get close and relax her for when they returned to the cottage.

"Sure. You have first go at the shower and I'll call."

The restaurant occupied half of the second floor of a building that housed a block of storefronts. Wide windows looked out onto the rainy night and the cozy lights of the cottages across the highway. Beyond them was the roaring ocean, the beam from Yaquina Bay lighthouse the only thing visible in the dark vastness.

Several dozen tables topped with pink tablecloths and gleaming hurricane lamps filled the room, except for a small space in the corner. A live band sat on a low dias, leaving room for a dance floor not much bigger than the bathroom off Ben's bedroom at home.

Those taking advantage of it at the moment didn't seem to mind, though, he thought, as he watched couples pressed tightly together and gazing into each other's eyes.

The waiter led Natalie and Ben toward a table by a window, lowered the wick on their lamp and left them with menus almost bigger than the dance floor.

Natalie hid behind hers for some time.

"Anything look good?" Ben asked finally.

He could see only her eyes above the top of the menu.

"I was thinking about steak," she said, her head tipped back so that she could see him above the obstruction. "I haven't had red meat in ages. I'll make up for it by skipping dessert."

"I thought you weren't going to diet on this trip."

"I'm just trying to be sensible," she replied. "And I don't want to be..." She hesitated, a stricken look in her eyes as what she'd apparently been about to say gave her second thoughts.

That was it. He decided it would be easier on both of them if he made her admit her nervousness.

He leaned across the table toward her, lowering his voice. "You're afraid red meat will make you stronger than I can handle?"

She looked first upset that he'd brought up the issue, then resigned to the fact that it should be faced.

"No, I was afraid I'd get sleepy," she admitted.

He grinned. "You're not giving me much credit. I think I can keep you interested and awake."

She scolded him with a look. "We're not doing this because of your prowess."

He arched an eyebrow in surprise. "I thought we were. Or, at least, my desirability as a baby—"

"Stop!" She put a hand up, looking a little like one of the Supremes in the middle of "Stop in the Name of Love."

For a moment he had the horrible impression that she'd changed her mind about the entire plan. And while he did truly want her to do what she considered best for herself, he was getting into the idea of making love to her and fathering her baby.

He'd enjoyed every minute he'd spent with her today, from long conversations in the car about her work and his girls, to sight-seeing with her and discovering her enjoyment in everything and her reporter's thirst to know more.

It made him want to know more about her—the

kinds of things a man learned about a woman only when he made love to her.

He sat quietly, sanity and libido delicately balanced as he waited for her to explain.

"Have I made you feel like a...an object?" she asked.

It was such a dramatic question that it amused him, yet she seemed entirely serious. So he was careful not to smile.

"I mean, as though you have nothing to do with this except as a—a..."

"A sperm donor?" he asked softly, mercilessly. He'd agreed to do this for his own purposes, but it was an opportunity to make a point.

She closed her menu, turned it sideways and looked at him over it, her expression apologetic.

"I'm sorry," she said, shaking her head regretfully. "I'm sorry. That's still what it all boils down to, isn't it? I didn't really think about that until you said earlier today that you understood I was indulging my wish to have a baby and not a man. Then I realized how you must feel—used, probably, simply because you're handsome and well built and have the kind of personality I'd like my baby to have."

He didn't feel any of the things she was worried about. And it was certainly hard to find any problem with her perception of him.

"You didn't tie me up and put me in the car, did you?" he asked. "Although, if you'd like to reconsider and try that, it could be fun."

She seemed pleased that he'd insisted he hadn't been forced, then annoyed that he'd joked about it.

"I'm here because I want to be," he said plainly. "I like being with you. I'm looking forward to making love to you. But if you've never made love to someone with whom you've connected emotionally, then you might want to think twice about it—not because of how it might hurt me in any way, but because of how it might change you."

She blinked at him. "I'm not looking to...connect," she said. "I just want a baby."

He smiled, not surprised that she hadn't even noticed it was too late to claim that. She studied everything around her, but he wondered how long it had been since she'd taken a good look at herself.

Not that he was wild about their *connection,* either, but at least he'd connected before and knew what to expect.

"Right," he agreed. "It's just that what you expect to happen is often very different from what really happens when your emotions are involved."

"But they aren't," she insisted.

Maybe, he decided, it was safer to let her believe that. He turned his attention back to his menu.

"Okay. I'll have steak, too, to make sure I'm prepared," he said. "And the smoked oyster appetizer."

She reached across the table to bend his menu back so that she could look into his face. "Ben. You're not going to...get hurt here, are you?"

He wasn't sure yet. It was looking as though that was entirely possible. "No," he lied. "My heart's still under wraps."

She smiled with relief. "Good." Then she looked horrified. "Oh, I didn't mean good that you're—"

He raised his hand to cut her off. "I know what you meant. It's all right. We're just two people getting together to make a baby. A very simple equation."

She began to nod, smiling again, then her expression changed abruptly to grave seriousness.

"What?"

"You said it's a very simple equation," she repeated, her eyes meeting his. "But it's not."

"Why not?"

"Because in this instance, one and one makes...three."

The waiter arrived, suspending their discussion. As Natalie placed her order, Ben thought calmly that she was right. This was going to be a relationship that defied even the laws of mathematics.

Chapter Eight

Natalie found dancing with Ben filled with contradictions. He held her loosely, yet she found herself pressed tightly against him, every muscled plane of his body fitting comfortably into the soft hollows of hers.

She was prepared to blame it on the tight confines of the dance floor, but looked around and realized that there were only two other couples dancing. She, however, had her arms tightly wrapped around Ben's neck. So she was to blame.

She felt nervous, yet eager. She wished she'd never suggested this, then wished their paths had crossed before she'd ever tried the sperm bank. Her life would be much simpler now.

Or would it? Nothing seemed simple at the moment. As the band played a smooth romantic arrangement of ''Autumn Leaves,'' she could feel her heartbeat in her ears. She remembered her insistence that her feelings weren't involved here, and wondered why she'd thought so.

Because he hadn't been holding her when she'd said it, that's why. She'd had this reaction to him when she was injured and he'd lifted her in his arms to move her from place to place. When they simply talked, she could be sensible and steady. When they touched, every nerve ending in her body seemed to come alive.

"You okay?" he asked gently.

She lifted her head from his shoulder to look into his eyes. "Yes. Why?"

The hand splayed against her back pressed gently. "Because you don't seem to be breathing."

She admitted with a shallow little breath, "I'm nervous."

"No need to be," he assured her quietly. "I'm harmless."

"Yeah," she said with a disbelieving purse of her mouth. "Right."

"You changing your mind?" he asked with a smile. "I know you've had your red meat to strengthen you and wine to relax you, but you're in no way obliged to carry through. There's tomorrow, or the day after, or never. Everything's up to you."

And that was probably what did it, she decided later. So little in her life had ever been up to her. Most of her life had pretty much been up to her mother, and even when Natalie had resisted, her peace of mind had been subject to her mother's reactions.

In her work, the way in which the news was presented was up to the station management, and her position as anchor of the nightly news was subject to every whim and complaint of the viewing audience.

But this—making her baby—was up to her.

And she was ready. Or, rather, she knew it was do

it now or lose her nerve. It was all more complicated than she'd imagined, more…involving that she'd anticipated. She blamed her sudden emotional turmoil on the tension of the moment, on knowing that sometime tonight she would go back to the little cottage on the bluff and she and Ben would, hopefully, create her child.

It was a staggeringly important step in her life, so naturally her body reacted with the drama appropriate to the situation.

She stopped dancing, her hands slipping from around his neck to his shoulders. "I'd like to go back to the cottage," she whispered, "and…" She stumbled over the right way to put it. Several more couples had come onto the floor and she was trying to be discreet.

Ben didn't seem to need more words. "All right. Let's go."

He took her hand and led her back to the table for her purse, to the cloakroom for her coat, then out the door.

The fresh air, smelling of rain and the outdoors, followed them into the cottage, lending a chill to the warmth of the room.

"I'll go change," she said, snatching the black peignoir she'd left on the foot of the bed and hurrying into the bathroom. She closed the door and almost collapsed against it, wondering why in heaven's name she couldn't relax.

This was all her idea, she *wanted* to do it, Ben was wonderful and he'd just left the unfolding of the night in her hands.

What was her problem?

She pulled the black knit dress up over her head, dispensed with slip, stockings and undies, and shrugged into the silky, spaghetti-strapped nightie. Then she stood in the glare of the tiny room and breathed hard.

"I know you can do this," she told herself bracingly. "I just hope you can do it with some semblance of style."

Certain that stalling any longer would be fatal to her determination, she walked out of the bathroom, doing her best to look comfortable.

Ben had removed his clothes and wore a short, dark blue silk robe that fell to midthigh. He paced near the window, his cell phone to his ear, his long, strong legs quickening her pulse. He'd turned off the bedside lights, and the small lamp on the dresser lent a soft glow to the corner of the room nearest the door.

"Yeah, we saw the sea lions and the otters," he was saying. "And the undersea exhibit they were building when we were here makes it feel like you're swimming with the sharks." He listened a moment and turned to acknowledge Natalie with a small wave as she hung up her dress and put her underthings in the laundry bag that had been provided. "Yeah, it is cool. Natalie's favorite thing? I don't know. Why don't you ask her? Hold on."

He handed Natalie the phone. "Vanessa wants to know what you liked best about the aquarium."

"Hi, Vanessa," she said, sitting on the edge of the bed while Ben lounged in the barrel chair beside it.

"Hi!" Vanessa and Roxie chimed in unison.

"Daddy says you guys are having fun!" Vanessa sounded just a little jealous. "I wish we coulda gone to the aquarium, too."

"It was wonderful." Natalie felt herself relax just a little at the sound of the children's voices. "I loved everything, but I think I liked the otters the best. One was floating on his back and eating a shellfish off of his stomach. He was very cute."

"We're gonna watch *The Little Mermaid* before we go to bed," Roxie said. "What are you gonna watch?"

"Um…" Natalie had one moment of total fluster, then replied briskly, "Well, it was a long day. We'll probably just go right to bed. Do you want to talk to your dad again?"

"Yes, please," Vanessa replied.

"Okay. Good night, you two. Sleep tight." She walked around the bed and handed the phone to Ben. He caught her hand when she would have walked away.

"You guys be good for Grandma, okay?" he said. There was excited conversation on the other end, then he added, "Of course we'll bring you presents. I love you. Okay. Good night, Vanessa. Good night, Roxie."

Ben hit the close button on the phone and put it on the nightstand. Then he tugged Natalie gently down into his lap.

"I thought you might want to sit with me," he said, wrapping his arms around her, "before you go to bed with me."

Natalie looked at him, her head a little higher than

his so that she looked down into his eyes and onto the strong line of his nose. A move calculated on his part, she guessed, to make her feel more in control.

Hearing him talking on the phone to his girls did relax her considerably, she realized. He was a great dad, she reminded herself, as well as the amusing companion he'd been all day, and the sizzlingly sexy man he'd been this evening.

"I'm going to make myself your manager," she said, resting her head on his shoulder, "and take you on the road."

"Ah…" he said with theatrical reluctance, "you haven't seen me perform yet."

She slapped his chest. "I meant that I'd take you on the road to give guy lessons to other men."

"Really."

"Yes. You're quite remarkable. Totally male without aggression or intimidation."

He laughed softly. "At the moment, anyway."

"We'll make the world a happier place."

"I'm for that."

She heaved a sigh and basked in the comfort and security of the cradle of his arms. "How long can I stay like this?"

"Until you're ready to move on."

"You're very generous."

"It's all part of the 'Being a Guy' program."

She laughed and kissed his cheek because she simply felt compelled. And there was something about the prickle of the beginnings of beard against her lips, of the warmth of his skin, of the muscle in his jaw that moved against her cheek, that changed him back again from gentle father to dangerous male.

And something elemental in her responded to that with excitement rather than fear.

He turned his head to look into her eyes, his lips now aligned with hers.

Mesmerized, she waited for him to kiss her, but he didn't. His eyes roved her face in apparent fascination, and the hand on her knees that held her in his lap tightened considerably. His head tilted, his lips parted, but he made no move to close the small space between them.

Then she understood. He'd said every forward move was up to her. So she made it, putting her mouth to his, feeling his warmth, his instant, enthusiastic response.

He kissed her chin, her throat, her ear, then her lips again, his mouth clever and avid as the hand on her knee inched upward under the hem of her negligee.

Her pulse accelerated and her lungs stopped working altogether. She finally drew her mouth away and gasped for air. "Ben!" she whispered.

"Yes?" he asked as his hand moved higher and his mouth dipped to the hollow of her throat.

She pointed backward toward the bed, unable to concentrate on forming of words.

"In a minute," he replied, pulling her closer to him.

She felt a brief moment of halfhearted indignation because she was supposed to be directing this. Then his hand roved over her hip and followed the curve of her bottom, and she forgot her complaint as desire heated her body.

He stood with her in his arms and placed her on the bed. After he made a quick detour to turn off the light on the dresser, she heard the slither of silk that meant he'd rid himself of the robe.

He was beside her again, taking her into the curve of his arm, his free hand roving over her through the gown, exploring breast, stomach, thigh.

She ran her hands up his back, felt strong muscle and sharp angles and heard the intake of his breath as her hands dipped to the small of his back.

He rolled over, pulling her astride him, gathered up the hem of her negligee and pushed it up her body. She caught it from him and pulled it off, tossing it over the side of the bed.

She'd never been uppermost in making love before, but she dismissed her momentary alarm because of her new trust in him and, inexplicably, a new trust in herself.

Ben moved slowly. His hands covered her small, firm breasts and he delighted in the beading of their tips in his palm. He loved the way her head tipped backward and her lips parted as he ran his thumbs over her pearled nipples, then skimmed his fingertips down her sides to her waist, tracing a finger across her abdomen.

She caught his forearms and held on to them, not to stop him, but as though she needed their solidity for balance.

She said his name in a startled whisper, seeming surprised by…what? He wasn't sure.

He caught her hips in his hands and she groaned aloud, leaning forward to kiss him, nipping at his bottom lip, his chin, his collarbone.

She dotted kisses across his chest, down the middle of his ribs to his navel, moving dangerously low.

He caught her arms and pulled her up the length of his body.

"I thought I was in charge here," she teased softly, planting kisses in his ear.

"Yes," he replied, feeling drunk on her charms, "but I'm in charge of the pleasure."

"You're doing very, very well," she praised thickly.

He swept a hand down her back, hitched her leg up and reached tenderly inside her.

She gasped audibly and lay still against him, whispering his name again.

Old pain inside him melted a little every time he heard it.

In seconds he'd turned her gasp into a cry. One of her hands caught a fistful of his hair, the other his shoulder, then she shuddered against him, as much a part of him as his own skin.

NATALIE WAS SHAKEN, not simply by the delicious fulfillment, but because he'd given it to her. It wasn't required for the baby-making process.

Baby-making. For a time there, it had almost slipped her mind that that was what they were doing. But his hands on her body seemed to make all kinds of things slip her mind.

She raised her head to look into his face, the darkness robbing it of any detail except the white of his smile.

He raised a hand to brush the hair out of her eyes.

"I'm reclaiming control," she said, catching his forearms in her hands and pushing them out to his sides. "And I don't want any opposition."

"But you—"

"Or discussion." She silenced him with a kiss that eventually moved from his lips down the middle of his body to the objective she'd had earlier when he'd stopped her.

HIS INTENTION TO MAKE HER comatose with pleasure before entering her was derailed the instant she touched him.

"Nat..." he began, intent on sitting up. But she pushed him back with her index finger in the middle of his chest.

"I asked you to be quiet," she said, putting her lips to him and almost sending him over the edge.

He was vaguely aware of moving to accommodate her as she positioned herself over him, of taking her hips in his hands and entering her gently as she came down on him.

Then he lost all good sense as his body reacted instantly to the tight enclosure of hers.

Release for the first time in over eighteen months was so exquisite, it was almost pain. He felt scrubbed, raked, sanded. And then a blissful contentment was forced into him, pore by pore, as she collapsed atop him, her breasts and the slight jut of her ribs pushing into his chest.

"Merciful heavens, Ben!" she whispered, and a light went on inside him.

NATALIE CURLED INTO Ben's arm, her back to his chest, and knew something life-changing had happened.

"I have my baby," she whispered to herself.

"Whose baby?" Ben asked in her ear.

"Our baby," she corrected.

"Damn right."

THEY LEFT EARLY the following morning and drove to Yachats for breakfast.

Ben corrected her pronunciation of it. "It's not Ya-chats, it's Yaw-hots."

"Where did *that* name come from?" she asked, looking through her brochure for it, but finding no answer.

"Not sure," he replied. "But I know a great restaurant there."

"Good." She folded her brochure and tucked it back into her purse. "I'm starving."

She felt as though her body was working overtime this morning. Her system seemed to be revved, a little internal tremor quaking from limb to limb and settling in her heart. Ben hadn't mentioned the night before, and since she wasn't entirely sure what to make of it, she hadn't, either.

So she chose not to think about it. He seemed to be determined to simply enjoy the day, so she followed his lead.

Ten minutes later he winced at her in disbelief.

They sat in a coffee shop built on rocks overlooking the beach. "You're actually having *blackberry pie à la mode* for breakfast?"

"You don't want me to watch my diet on this trip, remember?" She smiled blandly.

"You'll have an hour's worth of sugar high, then you'll crash like a one-winged airplane."

"No, I won't. And Oregon's noted for its blackberries. I have to try it."

"For breakfast."

"Yes."

It was scrumptious. She savored every bite, and when she'd finished she looked up from her plate to find Ben watching her with amused indulgence. The look touched her. She didn't remember ever amusing anyone, or getting that look that suggested you were somehow precious to the beholder.

"You want me to drive?" she asked, needing to say something quickly to break the spell.

He shook his head as he put several bills on the table. "And have you fall asleep with a long drop to the ocean on our right side? I don't think so."

She shrugged and took a last sip of coffee. "Fine. I'd rather be able to gawk out the window, anyway."

Outside, Ben unlocked her door and held it open for her.

"Thank you," she said, tossing her purse in. She reached up for the side handle, preparing to climb into the front seat.

"Hey." Ben caught her arm to stop her and turned her around.

She looked up at him in question just in time to

see his mouth come down on hers and kiss her with a tender passion that evoked the night before in all its velvet desire and wonder.

Her response was natural and immediate and rocked her considerably. She stammered a moment, then decided against saying anything, and climbed into the van.

Ben left the parking lot heading south, and the next thing Natalie knew, she opened her eyes to a rain-spattered window and a sign that read, Cape Perpetua, 18 Miles of Hiking Trails.

She *had* fallen asleep!

She sat up quickly and glanced guiltily his way.

"I think we'll have to pass on hiking anywhere," Ben said. "Maybe we'll have better weather for that on the way back."

"Good decision," she applauded.

"Which I made on my own," he pointed out with a grinning glance in her direction, "since you were *asleep.*"

"I was resting my eyes."

"Uh-huh."

"It wasn't the pie."

"Of course not."

"Perhaps," she said sweetly, "it was the four hours you kept me awake last night proving to me that…"

He sent her an interested glance. "Yes?"

"That…enthusiasm is essential to the task of baby-making."

The interest in his glance became a gleam of memory. "You seemed to catch on. But you'll notice that *I* didn't fall asleep."

"You'll probably be too tired to even eat dinner tonight," she predicted.

But she was wrong. He walked with her through the Sea Lion Caves north of Florence and through the gift shop while they searched for souvenirs for the girls. They took a ride on a stern-wheeler a little farther south, then visited the Siuslaw Pioneer Museum for pioneer and Native American history and looked at every exhibit.

When they finally found a motel in Reedsport, she was heavy-lidded with weariness. But he seemed as fresh as he had that morning.

She shoved him with playful resentment as she headed for the bed. "What's wrong with you, anyway?" she asked, falling onto it.

He leaned over her to cover her with the other half of the coverlet. "I've done physical work all my life," he replied, pulling her pillow down so that it fit just right into the notch at her shoulder. "I have a lot of endurance. Unlike some people who have wimpy desk jobs and eat pie for breakfast."

"You're a nag, Griffin," she said halfheartedly as her limbs began to relax.

"Sweet-talker," he said.

The room was dark when Natalie awoke. She sat up in momentary alarm, disoriented.

Out of the dark, a hand caught her arm. "What's the matter?" Ben asked.

"Oh." She remembered suddenly where she was, and everything inside her grew warm with happiness.

"Hi, Ben." She fell sideways toward the sound of his voice. "Ha! You were *sleeping!* You're not Superman after all!" He was propped up on an elbow on his pillow, and she landed against him. He lowered his arm to touch her hair.

"Oh, Natty," he said, his tone suggesting retribution. "That's too bold an accusation for a man to ignore."

"You were *sleeping.*"

"I wasn't. I was lying here beside you, watching *you* sleep."

"In the dark?"

He pointed to the window, where moonlight streamed in, the clouds that had plagued them all day finally gone.

"You're very beautiful with moonlight on your face," he said, his index finger tracing the line of her nose, touching her mouth with paralyzing tenderness, running over her chin and down her throat to trace a breast through her sweatshirt.

This tender caressing was beginning to worry her, his gentle affection more than she'd expected. "You don't have to say things like that," she said quietly. "I don't expect—"

The hand that had traced her profile now rose to land gently over her mouth. "Don't say another word," he warned, "or I'm going to get angry and lose the spirit to prove you wrong about the Superman crack."

His eyes in the moonlight told her he was teasing, but that she should be careful.

He lowered his hand to unfasten the button on her cords and tug the zipper down.

"I just don't want you to think you have to—" she began.

The hand covered her mouth again. "One more word," he threatened, "and I'll leave you here to sleep, go to dinner without you and not make love to you at all."

She drew his hand down. "This must be one of the bad qualities you tried to tell me you had," she said. Unfortunately, when she lowered his hand, she placed it over her breast so that now she couldn't remember the point she'd been trying to make, or the words he'd spoken.

"Do you want to argue?" he asked in a whisper, his mouth coming down to tantalize hers without actually settling on it as his hand moved artfully on her. "Or do you want to make love?"

She wrapped her arms around his neck and forced his mouth to make contact with hers.

An hour later she lay against him, breathing heavily.

"Okay," she conceded on a gasp. "You are Superman. Can we go to dinner, please? I'm sure we've burned every calorie in our bodies. Possibly even tomorrow's allotment."

"All right." He tossed the blankets back and pinched her hip as she swung her legs over the side of the bed. "Just be careful what you say."

She yelped, then smacked him with her pillow. He dodged it, caught her arm, and they ended up on the mattress again, a laughing tangle of arms and legs.

It was another hour before they got to dinner.

They made love that night and again the next morning, and rented a room a mere thirty miles away because by midmorning, they couldn't wait to make love again.

Ben decided, as he showered afterward, that he had to slow down here or he would be dead before he hit thirty-six. And Natalie would never live to be a mother.

He tried to bring Julie to mind but couldn't. The only pictures that would form in his brain were of Natalie—Natalie smiling, Natalie arguing, Natalie astride him in the throes of climax.

He was consumed with her. She fit perfectly in his arms; his body was made for hers. They enjoyed every moment of everything they did together—even when they disagreed. Life had a freshness he'd thought he'd never see again.

But what was *she* thinking? he wondered. He knew she was as surprised and happy about their compatibility as he was. But he wasn't sure what it meant to her beyond helping her conceive a child.

They should talk about this, but he didn't want to do anything to upset this delicious equilibrium. She was relaxed and happy, and he was…well, *relaxed* certainly didn't describe it, but he was happy, too.

He knew it was irresponsible and immature to put off planning for what might happen when their trip was over, but he felt anything but responsible and adult. And he'd always dealt with what life gave him.

He just hoped with everything in him that it was giving him Natalie.

Chapter Nine

"There's an historical museum," Natalie said, her nose in a brochure as they passed each other in the bathroom doorway. She was wearing only her sweatshirt, and her hair was still mussed from their lovemaking, her cheeks pink. "An art museum, and a twenty-five-mile drive through old-growth myrtlewood groves."

He had put on his jeans, but still had a towel around his neck to dry his hair. "You want to do it all?" he asked, praying that she'd say no to the museums. He always found things to learn and enjoy in them, but he was a little edgy this morning and didn't relish the thought of having to move quietly from exhibit to exhibit, trying to absorb information. His brain was too beleaguered.

"I was thinking we should buy some sandwiches," she said, smiling up at him, "and move on. There are more myrtle trees at Myrtle Point, so we won't miss anything. And maybe we'll find a comfortable place to picnic. What do you think?"

He leaned down to kiss the tip of her nose. "I think

that sounds like a plan. But it's November. We might have to eat in the car.''

She put her hands on her hips. ''I thought you were used to working outdoors and considered *me* the hothouse flower?''

''I just don't want you to catch cold at the wrong moment.''

''You bought me a hat,'' she reminded him. ''And I'm generally strong as a horse.''

''All right, then. Don't take forever, okay?''

''I never take forever.''

''It took you an hour to get ready this morning.''

''I put on makeup.''

He took two steps back to look at her closely. ''You did?''

She leaned against the half-open door and batted her eyelashes playfully. ''For all the good it did me.''

He barked a scornful laugh. ''Please. If I was any more aware of you, we'd be up on charges somewhere for lewd behavior in public.''

She looked amused for about a heartbeat, then she looked worried. She finally closed the door, shouting, ''I'll be out in fifteen minutes.''

It was more like thirty, but she looked wonderful in a big pink sweater and black leggings, and he chose not to quibble. They found a deli on the main street, bought sandwiches, pasta salads and soft drinks, and climbed into the car to continue their journey south.

''Oh, there, Ben!'' she cried half an hour later when she spotted a fairly low wall of rocks running from the beach into the ocean. ''Want to picnic there?''

"Can you get out there on your ankle?" he asked.

"Sure. It hardly hurts at all anymore."

He parked on the side of the road and reached into the middle seat for their lunch.

She was already out of the car, pulling on her hat and heading across the sand to the rocks. She stepped carefully onto a flat-topped rock, then worked her way to a sort of trail along the top of the wall that had probably been worn into it by generations of feet looking for the perfect spot to picnic.

Ben followed, trying to keep an eye on her while watching his own footing.

She went to the very end, about thirty feet out, where a large flat boulder provided perfect seating.

The wind was so cold that he pulled his own hat on and turned up his collar.

"Isn't this invigorating?" she asked, clearly thrilled with their spot. Her legs dangled over the side, the backs of her shoes bumping rhythmically against the rock.

"Yes, it is," he replied. "It reminds me of working outside in February in Fairbanks."

She laughed and punched his arm. "It isn't that bad. All this good oxygen will help us think clearly."

He dug into the bag and handed her a can of pop. "About what?"

"About what to do if I am pregnant," she replied casually, but he heard the subtle change in her voice.

"We've already agreed on that," he reminded her, handing her a paper cup of pasta salad. "You're staying until we know, then if you are, you're staying until the baby's born."

She made a production of removing the plastic lid. "I was just wondering how practical that is."

She was hedging—or reneging; he wasn't sure which. He just knew he wasn't tolerating either.

"How practical is any of this?" he asked.

"I'm supposed to be back at work in a few weeks."

He pulled the top off his pop, took a long pull, then asked candidly, "You're not thinking I'm going to let you ignore our agreement?"

"No." She dipped her fork into the salad, took one miniscule bite, then said, her eyes turning toward him with what seemed to be reluctance, "I am thinking that it's all becoming…important. Urgent, even."

"Of course it's important. It's a baby."

"I don't mean the baby." She took another bite of salad, then capped the cup and put it back into the bag he held. She wrapped her arms around herself and stared at the bright horizon. "I mean us."

Us.

He rested his pop can in a space between two rocks and gave himself time to answer by reaching into the bag for her sandwich and handing it to her.

"You mean we've become important to you." He had to make sure he was clear on that.

She looked uncertain. "Am I the only one that's happening to?"

"No," he replied quickly, firmly. "I'm just not as surprised as you are. I warned you about this, remember?"

She made a mildly disapproving face. "Nice of you to say 'I told you so.'"

"Sure." He had to laugh despite her seriousness. "I learned it from my mother."

"I was also thinking," Natalie said after a cautious pause, though she bravely held his gaze, "that it might be wise if I left now, before it becomes too hard to leave. I know how you feel about being a long-distance father, but what if I promise—"

"No," he said simply.

She uttered an indignant little gasp. "You don't think we should discuss it?"

"No."

"You don't think I should have a say in—?"

"You had your say," he reminded her. "You asked me to father your baby and I've done my damnedest to make that happen. And I told you I wouldn't let you run off with it."

"But we don't know…"

He shrugged. "No, we don't. Not for sure. But the deal was you stayed until we did."

She put a hand to her stomach, as though she had some sixth sense that told her she *was* pregnant even while they fought about it.

"You'll hate me if you feel…stuck with me," she warned.

"Does anything in my treatment of you," he asked wryly, "suggest that I hate you?"

"I'm talking six months down the road."

"I'm steady—solid. Today or six months from now, I'll feel the same. I think you're the unknown quantity here."

She hitched a knee up on the rock to turn her body

toward him. He reached out to steady her on their somewhat precarious perch.

"I'm also steady and solid," she said a little testily. "I know the condition I was in the first time you saw me didn't show me off to best advantage, but I'm usually a very responsible person. And that's the point I'm trying to make."

He gave her his full attention. "Then you'll have to be more clear."

"If I go home now, and I'm not pregnant, then you haven't lost anything. I'm the only one who didn't get what I wanted."

"I'm with you so far."

"But if I am, I promise you I'll love and care for this baby with everything in me and you won't have to have your whole life disrupted...."

Clever woman. Carefully calculated argument. But Ben honed his debating skills regularly with Vanessa and Roxie.

"Natalie," he said, "you have already disrupted my entire life with this scheme. And the problem you're not considering is that while I refuse to let you put three thousand miles between us before we know whether or not you're pregnant, the baby's not the only issue for me."

She nodded. "I know. There's health insurance, education, all those—"

"No," he said again. Sometimes she was so thick. "I mean I'm falling in love with you."

LOVE.
Love.

He was falling in love with her.

Natalie heard the words with warring emotions of terror and delight. She'd longed for years to hear a man tell her he loved her. She dreamed about it asleep and awake.

Then, when Kyle had said it but not meant it, she'd decided she would simply live without it. And that had had its advantages.

She liked doing only what she wanted to do, answering to no one, explaining to no one.

But with Ben Griffin in her life, those days would be gone forever—and then some.

If she was forced to be honest, though, she was a little bit in love with him, too. And she knew he was the kind of man accustomed to taking charge. He didn't have despotic tendencies; he just thought he knew what should be done and did it. Still, that wouldn't be easy to live with for a woman who'd decided she liked her autonomy.

And this baby was supposed to be *hers*—hers to love, someone to love her in return.

"Falling in love," she said, repeating his words, "isn't *completely* being in love. It could change on you."

He denied that with a glance. "What did I just tell you about me?"

She sighed. "That you're steady and solid. I know. But love can be a fleeting thing. It comes and goes, it runs hot and cold...."

He frowned at her assessment. "No, it doesn't. Infatuation comes and goes, and people run hot and cold. Love that's honestly formed and carefully nurtured is as dependable as the rock we're sitting on.''

"You said you weren't looking for a wife."

He hesitated a fraction of a second. "Yeah. I wasn't.''

She blinked at him. "You're telling me you've changed your mind? Would a steady and solid man do that in twenty-four hours' time?"

She thought she had him there, but he smiled softly with a self-deprecating look that made it hard to flaunt her victory. "Love is the only thing stronger than a steady, solid man. Or woman."

"I'm not in love," she said, able to convince herself that was true. "Not even a little bit," she added, but that was a fib. She thought she might be. Making a baby with him had none of the clinical aspects she'd originally imagined, and many of the dream elements she'd long ago abandoned in her attempt to be more realistic in her expectations.

He looked into her eyes, and she did her best to meet his gaze unflinchingly so he wouldn't suspect she was lying.

"Then," he said, taking the sandwich from her, unwrapping it and handing her half, "I guess you're the only one with something to worry about."

She tried to follow that line of reasoning and failed. "How's that?"

"Because I'm falling in love, and love decides the rules. So I can be big enough to let you go, if that's what I have to do."

"And what do you think I'll be worrying about?"

He chewed a bite of his sandwich. "You won't

know what to do,'' he said easily, ''because you won't know how to decide. If you use reason, the logical move would be to stay with your baby's father. If you decide selfishly, you'll do what's best for you.'' He looked into her eyes and said with gentle confidence, ''But you're not selfish by nature, so that'll bother you. And you still won't know what to do.''

''How do you know I'm not selfish?'' she demanded, confused by his logic. ''I've just used you for my own purposes.''

Now there was a smile in that gentle confidence. ''You didn't use me at all. You gave to me, you spoiled me, you were playful and wild and very, very generous with me. I know you now, Natty.''

She shook her head at him. ''Well, I'm glad you know me, because I don't recognize me anymore. I know you're a wonderful father and that you were a wonderful husband—but you told me you still loved Julie.''

''I'll always love Julie,'' he replied, his voice lowering in pitch and volume. ''But there seems to be more room in my heart than there used to be. And I know you don't want to hear this, but I think you've done that.''

Instead of comforting her, those words served only to expand Natalie's panic. She'd been searching for years for the right man, and she and Ben had known each other just a week. This enormous feeling she had inside her had to be the result of the importance of making a baby. It simply paralleled the scope of the change it would make in her life.

It wasn't love.

It couldn't be love.

She decided against it. She wouldn't know what to do with it.

And—what frightened her most—she wouldn't be able to handle it.

BEN READ THE PANIC in her eyes and decided it was time to cut her some slack. "Eat your sandwich," he said. "It's not as though we're sure you're pregnant. Or that what we do about us is something we have to decide this minute. Even if you are pregnant, we have until the baby comes to make our plans."

She cast him a dark glance. "I know, but now you have me worrying about it."

He opened his mouth to reassure her, but she misinterpreted his intentions. "Right, right. You warned me this wasn't going to be as easy and as problem free as I thought."

"I was going to say that I promise not to bring it up again until then, as long as you promise not to talk about leaving again. Unless you're not pregnant, then I guess I have to let you go whether I want to or not."

She looked conflicted. He guessed she was wondering whether to hope she was or *wasn't* pregnant.

He accepted grimly that their delicious lovemaking was over. She was probably deciding to take her chances on what they'd "accomplished" already.

They had dinner in Brookings, within minutes of the California border. Their room, just steps from the ocean, had every convenience, including a private deck, a small, well-equipped kitchen and a hot tub.

Natalie suggested they cook in the room instead of going out for dinner. A quick trip to the grocery store yielded steaks and salad makings, a package of Ho-Ho's and a bottle of wine.

Ben prepared the salad while Natalie grilled the steaks. She'd relaxed a little, but wasn't quite the witty companion she was when nothing troubled her.

He took special pains to be congenial and helpful, without invading the space she'd walled around herself. He looked longingly at the hot tub, but kept his personal promise to leave the next step in their physical relationship up to her. He prepared himself to accept that it was over—at least until he had time to convince her otherwise.

The steaks were garlicky and delicious, his salad creative, with red cabbage and spinach added to romaine and topped with tomatoes, red and yellow peppers and green onions.

When they were finished, Natalie groaned. "After this week, I'm going to *look* pregnant, whether I am or not."

He laughed. "Most men appreciate curves. I wouldn't worry about it. I'll get dessert," he volunteered a moment later.

She caught his arm when he would have stood. "I was thinking we could take the rest of the wine and the Ho-Ho's into the hot tub. *The Mummy* is on at eight o'clock and we can see the television from the tub."

There was a sparkle in her eye at the prospect of a scary movie under such decadent conditions.

He reacted with enthusiasm, though watching a movie wasn't the best use of a hot tub that he could think of.

He poured two glasses of wine and put the Ho-Ho's on a plate while she disappeared into the bathroom.

He came out with a tray to find her in a robe, fiddling with controls as she filled the tub.

"Medium hot or hot?" she asked.

"Medium," he replied. "If it isn't hot enough, we can add more."

She tested the rising water with her hand and nodded in satisfaction. "See what you think."

He handed her the tray and dipped his hand in. "Perfect," he said.

"Good." She put the tray on the broad edge of the tub, unselfconsciously pulled off her robe and stepped into the water. "Hurry up," she advised with a grinning glance at him, "or I'm eating all the Ho-Ho's."

Momentarily paralyzed by the sight of her beautiful body slipping into the ripples of water, and not entirely sure what was happening here, he still managed to shed his clothes where he stood. He believed her about the Ho-Ho's.

For the first hour, she leaned against him in easy intimacy, drinking wine and eating dessert as the adventurer and the librarian in the film tracked down a sacred book while being pursued by a vengeful mummy.

Ben put a casual arm around her shoulders and let

her hide her face against him when the mechanical scarabs attacked.

During a commercial break, she pulled on her robe, ran for a towel for him and hurried into the kitchen.

He groaned quietly as he shrugged into his robe, his libido stronger than his patience. But he propped up their pillows against the headboard of the bed and turned the television slightly.

"Movie!" he shouted toward the kitchen when it began again.

She bustled in with a tray bearing two cups of coffee and packaged cream and sugar. They placed it between them on the bed until the powerful mummy breathed a cloud of locusts onto a crowd of villagers. Then he had to move it hurriedly when she scrambled closer to hide her face again.

"Why do you love scary movies," he asked in amusement, "when you can't watch them?"

"I watch most of them," she replied, her voice muffled against his robe. "I just don't like the bloody stuff. Or the really creepy parts. It's a little like you dancing so well, but not liking to do it."

He thought that through and decided it didn't compute. "It's not like that at all," he argued.

She put a hand over his mouth. "I can't hear the television. Can't you just let me be right?"

"Not if you're wrong," he replied softly, nipping at her fingers.

She giggled and settled into the curve of his shoulder now that the scene had changed.

When the movie was over, she cleared away their

things and together they did the few dishes and tidied up the kitchen.

Ben put the lights out and they shed their robes and went to bed. Ben stayed on his side and she remained carefully on hers.

"Is it supposed to rain tomorrow?" she asked after a few moments.

"I don't know," he answered. "I didn't hear a report today."

"I suppose we should head home tomorrow."

"If you'd like time to gamble and visit the discount mall, we should."

She sighed. "I don't think I do. I've loved just watching the ocean and listening to the trees and the birds. Oregon has music as well as perfume."

Yes. He'd always thought so.

"Or we could stay here one more night," she proposed. "Just walk the beach tomorrow, cook our meals here, sit in the hot tub." She added with what sounded like a smile, "I loved the hot tub."

"Maybe we can find more scary movies," he suggested. "I like protecting you from the creepy parts."

She was up against him in an instant, her arm flung vehemently around his chest. "Ben!" she whispered. The smile had apparently turned to tears in an instant. He felt them against his chest. "What are we going to do?"

He knew she wasn't talking about whether or not to leave tomorrow.

"We don't have to do anything for a while," he assured her, wrapping his arms around her and holding her close. "We talked about it on the rocks, remember?"

"I remember, but I can't fall in love with you all the way. I just can't."

All the way? That suggested she was in love with him part of the way. He knew it would drive her crazy if he didn't ask why.

"Don't you want to know why?" she asked.

He felt her head rise off his chest. She looked down on him, her pale eyes pooled with tears in the darkness.

"I know why," he said, framing her face in his hands and wiping a tear away with his thumb. "You don't trust men. You've given them up."

"Smarty," she said, laying her head down again. "But there's more."

He stroked her hair, rubbed her back.

"Don't you want to know what?" she asked, a little impatiently this time.

"No," he replied honestly. "I'd like to hear a reason why you *can* fall in love with me."

"I don't have one of those," she said. "And the other reason I can't fall in love with you is the girls."

Before he could be offended, she added quickly, "Not because I don't love them to pieces. I do. But though my mother means well, she's pretty terrible as a role model. I don't know how to be a mother."

"Natty." He couldn't help the disbelief in his voice. "We're on this trip because you want a baby! What are you intending to be to it? A fairy godmother?"

"That's a baby!" she said emphatically, propping

herself on her forearms on his chest. "That's different. I can learn as I go. I've been reading books and I'll have time to get the hang of it before the baby starts asking important questions or needing me to know things besides how to feed and diaper him. Vanessa and Roxie need things now and I don't—"

"That's ridiculous," he interrupted. "Parenthood is ten percent common sense and ninety percent persistence. They just need straight answers and someone to make sure they apply them. And to keep them from killing themselves. That's important and something the books forget to tell you." When she still looked doubtful, he heaved a martyred sigh. "All right, then. I'll give them away."

With a huff of indignation, she rolled off him and onto her other side. "I'm spilling my guts and you're making jokes!" she accused.

He laughed, wrapped an arm around her and drew her back to him. "I'm sorry," he said, laying his cheek atop hers. "But that's such a silly reason, it's hard for me to take it seriously. You saw yourself how they fell in love with you right away. How easily you related to them."

"That's now. What about when I have to deny them something and become the wicked stepmother?"

"Then we'll give *you* away."

"You are so close to getting a smack," she warned.

"Okay, okay." He kissed her cheek. "I think the best thing to do is just relax about everything and live our lives. We don't know that you're pregnant, we don't know that we're going to fall *completely* in love, as you pointed out earlier...." He was already there, but it seemed wise not to share that right now. "Things have a way of working themselves out."

"I don't believe that," she insisted stubbornly. "I think people get messed up when they don't take an active part in deciding the direction of their lives. All they can do is react to what happens."

"In matters of business, where to live, who to vote for, maybe. But when the heart's involved, I think you should let it have its head."

"Hearts don't have a head. That's the problem."

He bit her earlobe punitively. She gasped.

"Let me rephrase. You should let it do what it wants because it usually makes the right decision."

"That hasn't been my experience," she quibbled.

"Loving Kyle wasn't a matter of the heart," Ben said brutally. "It was a matter of hormones. You wanted a baby and he was an eligible man who expressed an interest in you. Loving me, however, is."

He felt the tension leave her and her weight relax against him. "You were supposed to be just a babymaker, too," she said grudgingly. "And here I am...all mixed up."

He ran a hand gently down her side and over her hip.

"Well, if you're finding love confusing," he said quietly into her ear, "I could just take you for a love slave. That frees you from all those tedious questions of compromise and permanence."

She turned in his arms and wrapped hers around his neck. She was smiling again. He allowed himself a small sigh of relief.

"Are there wages involved?" she asked.

"Of course not. Slaves don't get wages."

"Then what's in it for me?"

"I don't sell you to somebody mean who doesn't like horror movies."

She nuzzled him. "How often would you need me?"

He kissed the line of her jaw. "You'd have to be available every day."

"I can do that," she agreed.

"All right," he said, wrapping an arm around her hips and pulling her even closer. "Show me."

Chapter Ten

Natalie and Ben stayed in Brookings an extra day, did all the things they'd talked about the night before, then drove straight home the following day.

Ben drove to his mother's to pick up the girls, while Natalie stayed home and started dinner. They'd picked up spaghetti makings and assorted vegetables for a plate of raw veggies and dip.

Vanessa and Roxie were delighted to be home again, and they were thrilled that Natalie was staying a few more weeks. They set the table for her while Ben went to check his phone messages.

"Grandma and some of her friends took us in-line skating!" Vanessa reported. "We had the best time! She said to ask you if you can make mince pie."

Natalie turned away from the stove, certain she'd misheard all of that.

"You went in-line skating with...Grandma?"

Both girls nodded. "Yeah."

"Grandma Lulu?"

"Yeah," Vanessa replied, apparently wondering why she was surprised. "Grandma Joanne is in Florida."

Natalie decided she could bring that picture into focus. Lulu was an original.

"And nobody broke any bones?"

"Grandma broke Mrs. Baldwin's dog leash when she went through it," Roxie relayed, dark eyes wide with excitement. "Mrs. Baldwin said a bad word, and Tippy fell on his back, but nothing happened to Grandma."

"Yeah," Vanessa corroborated. "Grandma caught the parking meter. We drove Mrs. Baldwin and Tippy home."

Natalie put both hands over her mouth, imagining the tangle of senior citizens and dog.

"And what about the mince pie?"

"It's for Thanksgiving," Vanessa explained. "Daddy likes it but nobody else does, so we usually have pumpkin. Grandma wants to know if you'll bring one to dinner."

"I've never made one before," Natalie admitted, "but I'm sure I can find a recipe." So Ben had told his mother she'd be staying for a while. She wondered what else he'd told her or what she'd concluded on her own. When the opportunity arose, Natalie thought, she should explain things to Lulu.

A woman youthful enough in her thinking to take two little girls in-line skating should understand about seeking a man's help to have a baby.

Ben appeared shortly afterward with a message written on a slip of paper. "Your cousin called while we were gone," he said, sniffing the air appreciatively. "She said to phone her and she'll take you to lunch."

Natalie felt a surge of warmth and well-being. The girls were happy, Ben seemed willing to let things develop between them without pressure of any kind, the holidays were coming and she had a kitchen project—mincemeat pie. Natalie loved the search for the right recipe, the right ingredients, and the hours spent in the kitchen preparing something special.

And Dori was home and wanted to meet for lunch!

Life was good.

"NATTY, I still can't believe you're here!" Dori said happily the following day as they walked arm in arm toward Burger's by the Sea. Natty had returned her call after dinner the night before and Dori had picked her up for lunch.

Dori hugged her fiercely, then drew back to look into her face. "You look wonderful, but...I don't know...different. But better, somehow." She frowned worriedly. "Mom told me about all that cruel publicity surrounding your sperm bank story. Sal and Max and I were in the Bahamas." She hugged her again. "I'm sorry I wasn't here when you needed me."

Natalie dismissed the publicity with a shake of her head. In her current exceptionally happy state, she wondered why it had upset her so. "I'm glad you and your family were having a wonderful time. Where is the baby?"

"Oh, Mom and Dad picked us up at the airport, and they've got all the preschool grandchildren at their place for a few days, so they kept Max and sent us home. Typical."

Natalie looped an arm in Dori's and walked her

inside. They ordered burgers, fries, onion rings and milk shakes.

"I can't believe you're eating like this," Dori chided as they slipped into a booth. "I thought the camera was unforgiving."

"It is, but I'm on leave for a few more weeks." She explained about finding the B-and-B when she'd learned Dori wasn't home, her disaster with cold pills and the strong toddy, and being taken home by Lulu's son.

Dori's eyebrows went up. "Who is Lulu's son?" she asked.

"Ben Griffin," Natalie replied. "He owns the Bijou Theater Building."

"You're kidding! I have a few friends with offices there. I've never crossed paths with him, though. What's he like?"

Natalie shrugged casually as the waitress put milk shakes in front of them. "Oh, you know. Handsome, charming, witty, great father, kind son, understanding friend. Your typical perfect man."

Dori laughed. "It's safe to say you're in love."

"A little bit," Natalie corrected.

"That didn't sound like just a 'little bit,'" Dori disputed. "That sounded like helplessly besotted." Then she pushed her milk shake aside to study her cousin's face closely. "Why do you want it to be just a little bit?"

Natalie explained that, too, by telling her about the arrangement she'd made with Ben, the trip they'd taken and his admission that he was falling in love with her.

"You know the kind of mother mine is," she said with a helpless spread of her hands. "I thought if I had a baby I could learn as it grows, but Ben's daughters are five and seven. We're buddies now, but what happens when they really need wisdom from me, or something I should know by simple maternal instinct? I don't have any. I never saw it in action."

"Natty." Dori reached across the table to pat her hand. "You're borrowing trouble. I had no baby experience and look at what happened to me. I had to learn and I did. And I don't think maternal skills are an inherited thing. The fact that your mom's..."

Natalie watched her cousin search for a diplomatic word. "I understand," Natalie said. "Just go on."

"It doesn't mean you won't be brilliant at it. I mean, kids are a little like reporters, aren't they? They're always asking 'what?' and 'why?' and they want every last detail. Well, you've got that sewn up. It's what you do so well that you've gotten awards."

Natalie caught her hand and squeezed it. She wasn't sure how accurate that analogy was, but being in Dori's company always made her feel better. "Thanks. I feel pretty panicky about the whole thing. Ben keeps telling me to relax, that we don't have to do anything about anything until we know whether or not I'm pregnant."

Dori grew sober. "I'm just playing devil's advocate here, but if you're *not* pregnant, what happens?"

"I'm not sure," Natalie replied frankly. "He loved his first wife very much, but he seems willing to start over." She sighed and played with the straw in her milk shake. "I just don't know how good I'd be at marriage, even if I could handle motherhood."

"If you're in love, you'll be good at marriage. And I think you'd be good at motherhood, whatever happened. You're always kind and fun to be with. That's the ideal mother right there."

"Thanks. I'd like to believe that." She leaned back as the waitress brought their burgers. "Anyway," she continued when they were alone again, "the deal we made was that if I did get pregnant, I'd stay here until the baby's born, then we'd decide about custody and hire a lawyer."

Dori nodded, smiling. "You have to admire a man who feels a sense of responsibility toward his baby."

"I do," she said with a dry twist to her lips. "It just complicates what I'd thought could be a simple and straightforward deal."

"There's nothing simple and straightforward about adding a child to your life."

Natalie laughed mirthlessly as she reached for the pepper. "So I've discovered."

BEN DECIDED THAT one of the many things he liked about Natalie's presence in his life was the aroma of dinner cooking when he came home from work. He knew it was a selfish, chauvinist reaction, but he couldn't help it. She was a wonderful cook, and while he'd valued his mother's casseroles like gold when he'd been in a hurry to put something on the table, he now came home to pork roast, lamb chops, baked chicken, and leftovers that were somehow as delicious as they'd been the first time—and he hadn't had to do anything but sit down at the table.

He lived a charmed life.

Now that he'd bought her a small used sport-utility vehicle, Natalie also picked up the girls from school so that he was able to work all afternoon. In one short week of an expanded work schedule, he'd been able to finish the office on the second floor and go over plans with an architect for turning the third floor space into apartments. The view from up there was spectacular and he had a feeling that four spacious apartments at a fair price would be snapped up in a hurry.

He went home midmorning the week before Thanksgiving to retrieve a tool he'd inadvertently left in the garage, and detected a wonderful aroma coming from the house.

Upon investigation, he found Natalie pouring brandy into a large pan of a gently bubbling stewish sort of concoction.

"What is that?" he asked, going to peer over her shoulder into the pot.

"Hi!" she said, stirring as she added another dab of his favorite brandy, Courvoisier. "Mincemeat," she replied, putting the bottle down and darting a guilty glance at him. "I'll replace the bottle for you, I promise. I got all the other ingredients required but forgot the brandy. Fortunately, you had a stash."

"Don't worry about it," he said, putting a hand on her shoulder to lean over her and take a deeper whiff. He couldn't quite believe it. "But why are you making it?"

"Your mother asked if I'd bring mince pie to

Thanksgiving dinner,'' she explained. ''She said it's your favorite.''

He kissed her cheek. ''Yeah, but I thought mince pie came from the grocery store freezer, or at best, from a jar on a shelf and a frozen pie crust.''

''I'm sure those are perfectly delicious,'' she said. ''I just love puttering in the kitchen. That's what I did all weekend when I worked. And I have to find something to do here. I'm just not used to this much downtime.''

He leaned an elbow on the counter and watched her stir. She wore a black-and-white apron designed to look like a tuxedo complete with white tie near the neck. Under it was a chambray shirt and stretch stirrup jeans. The sight of her in them always accelerated his pulse.

''You think you'll be bored if you are pregnant and have to stay here?'' he asked.

''I didn't say I was bored,'' she corrected, balancing her wooden spoon across the top of the pan. She lowered the heat and set the timer. ''I said I needed something productive to do. If I end up staying, I'll try to find a part-time job somewhere so I can still keep up the house and get meals.''

''You don't have to do that. I've told you before.''

''I like doing it.''

''Why?''

He guessed she hadn't really wanted to examine that, though it had been clear to him all week.

''Because it frees you up,'' she replied, wiping one hand on her apron while using the index finger on the other to follow the text of the recipe. ''And the girls enjoy helping me. I'm a people pleaser by nature, so we're all happy."

"And that explains it?" he prodded mercilessly. "A simple matter of personality satisfaction?"

She met his eyes and he saw the answer there, though he guessed she wouldn't say it.

"I haven't analyzed it," she admitted.

"But you're a reporter," he insisted. "You analyze everything else."

She picked up the wooden spoon and wielded it in a playfully threatening manner. "Did you come home simply to harass me?" she asked. "Or did you have another purpose?"

"I forgot a tool," he said. "I just threw it in the back of the van and smelled something cooking." He grinned. "Harassing you was just a perk. What's for dinner?"

"Cabbage rolls. When I drove the girls to school, they promised to try it. I told them if they can't handle the cabbage, they can just eat the innards and I'll fix them green beans or corn or something."

He shook his head at her. "You spoil them."

"And you don't? I don't know any other little girls who have custom-made, built-in beds made to look like Cinderella's carriage."

"Building's my job."

"And right now cooking is mine."

"Our baby," he said, straightening, "is going to have such a conflicted personality. Half you and half me, he won't be able to get along with himself."

She looked at him at that, and he was reminded of the time he'd disputed the gender change in Starla, and Vanessa had explained to him that only girls had stars in their eyes. He could see them now in Natalie's.

She looked a little awestruck, as though she'd just that moment realized that if she did carry a baby, it was part her and part him and not the faceless product of a lab.

She opened her mouth to speak, then simply expelled an exasperated gasp instead. "Aren't you meeting your architect for lunch?" she asked.

"Yes," he replied.

She pointed to his hands, greasy from the tool he'd retrieved. "You should wash up before you go. And don't mess with what's in the bathtub."

He stopped halfway to the bathroom off the kitchen. "What's in the bathtub?"

"Grapevines."

Of course. Grapevines. There were several very long ones soaking in hot water.

"There not going in the mincemeat, are they?" he shouted toward her as he washed his hands.

She laughed. "They're going to be wreaths—one for your front door and one for your mom's. After Thanksgiving, you can put Christmas decorations on them."

"Why are they soaking?"

"To make them pliable. Sort of like you steam wood."

He was just a little more amazed by her every day. "How come you know all this stuff?" He came back to her, drying his hands on a towel. "I thought career women were too busy for this sort of thing."

"I majored in communications in college," she replied, putting the seasonings she'd used back on their turntable in an overhead cupboard. "But I minored in home ec. Sundays are very long when you're single, so I'd pick out something to cook or some craft to explore. And I hated to vacation by myself, so I'd always pick one of those cooking vacations. I did Tuscany last year. It was wonderful."

"You're like some hybrid earth mother." He wondered why a woman with such talents had insecurities. "Do you enjoy your work in broadcasting?"

"On one level, I do." She closed the cupboard door and turned to face him. "I've met many important and exciting people, and there's never a dull moment in television. But I've often thought I'd love to have a Martha Stewart sort of show, but on a more practical level. You know—more for the mom in the Bronx than the matron on Long Island."

He could see that. "The Natalie Browning Show."

No. The Natalie Griffin Show. A small cable show out of Dancer's Beach, Oregon.

"Have you looked into the possibility? You must have all the connections."

"No." She turned away to put bowls and measuring cups in the dishwasher, her manner wistful. "It's just a pipe dream. Anyway, my life's in a state of flux right now."

Something was troubling her besides the direction of her professional future. He thought he could guess what it was.

"You have something to tell me?" he asked gently.

She was fussily rearranging cups in the top rack of the dishwasher and finally stopped to turn to him. She didn't look like a happy woman. *Oh, God,* he thought. *She's not pregnant and she's leaving.* Everything inside him seemed to sink.

She met his eyes, her own reluctant. "I'm late," she said quietly.

His first thought was that the words sounded so archaic, as though from a time when they sounded a death knell to social acceptance and to all dreams.

His second thought was relief that she wasn't leaving, followed instantly by excitement, and then concern that she didn't seem thrilled.

"Only a couple of days," she said, sounding close to tears. "But I took a test and it's..."

"Positive?"

"Yes."

He had no idea what was going on here. Julie had been complex, but they'd known each other since high school and they'd been friends before they were lovers.

Natalie, on the other hand, had been in his life about two and a half weeks in outrageously unusual circumstances. And she was always surprising him.

"I know it isn't definite until I see a doctor," she added, her voice barely audible. "But I think I'm pregnant."

He reached across the small space that separated them to draw her toward him. To his complete surprise, she flew into his arms and burst into sobs.

Okay. He'd had a lot of experience with tears with

all the women in his life. He simply held her and
waited.

"What have I *done* to your life?" she asked between sobs.

He rubbed a hand up and down her spine. "Only
good things, Natty," he replied, rocking her back and
forth. "I'm happy. Aren't you?"

She looked up at him in surprise, her face teary and
blotchy but somehow still beautiful. "I thought you
might be...upset."

"Why? This is what we agreed to do. And we did
it."

She scrubbed a hand over her eyes and pulled herself together. "What if I...what if I went home and
promised to come back when it's time for the baby
to be born?"

"No," he said.

"You'd have your life back."

She didn't seem to understand that she was becoming part of what made up his life. But maybe there
was something here that he wasn't getting.

"You miss Philadelphia?"

"No." She said it quickly, convincingly. "But I
have a contract I have to do something about. And
I'm just feeling..." She was dissembling on him
again. "Panicky. It was one thing when there was just
me involved, but now there's you and the girls and
to some degree your mom, and in my desperate, selfish need to have a baby I didn't understand...I mean,
I didn't feel..."

He pushed her onto the kitchen sofa and went to
pour her a brandy, then remembered that if she was

pregnant, that wasn't advisable. There was coffee in the pot, however, and he poured her a cup and added a teaspoon of sugar.

"There's no reason to feel panicky," he said, handing her the cup and sitting beside her. "Everything's going to be fine. We'll make an appointment with the doctor, and you can talk over all your concerns—"

"They're not physical concerns!" she interrupted tearfully, then took a deep sip of coffee. "They're— I guess—emotional."

He wanted to smile, remembering all the times she'd told him her emotions weren't involved. Wisely, he didn't.

"I'm going to be here until…" She paused to calculate.

"August," he said helpfully.

"Through winter," she said, "spring and most of summer. Can you deal with that?"

He replied soberly. "I'll do my best. Remember that you didn't force me into this."

"But you said no first," she reminded him in a tone of foreboding.

He shook his head at that. "Then I thought it over and changed my mind."

"Because my mother called and you felt sorry for me."

"No," he disputed firmly. "My feelings for you did not involve pity. Rampant fascination. Lust, maybe. But not pity. So stop worrying about me."

"How will we explain it to the girls?"

That was the tough one, but he'd managed tough explanations before.

"We'll be honest with them." He smiled. "You have to be because they always find you out."

Now she looked really worried. "You mean tell them that we're not married but I'm pregnant with their sibling and there's a possibility I'm going to be leaving with it in August?"

That possibility didn't exist, but he didn't think now was the time to tell her.

"You just have to pick and choose what to say and what to leave out unless they ask. Sometimes it works better than others, but usually I can make them comfortable with the issue, whatever it is."

She seemed willing to believe that.

"And your mom?"

"I'm sure she'll raise an eyebrow, but she's always supportive."

Natalie stared into the coffee, then finished it in one long gulp. She turned to him with a fragile smile. "You're sure you're happy?"

"Yes."

"What if we end up in *The Snitch* again?"

"I thought that was kind of exciting."

She focused on him suddenly, the caffeine taking effect as she became herself again. "You definitely *should* give guy classes. I think you could improve the lot of womankind single-handedly."

He accepted the compliment with a nod. "Right now, I'm just interested in you. You going to be all right if I go back to work?"

She nodded. "I'm sorry. I feel as though everything's racing around inside me. Hormones, I suppose. Did they make Julie crazy?"

They hadn't. She'd been a very serene pregnant woman.

"No." He got to his feet and offered Natalie a hand up. "She had food cravings, though. When she was pregnant with Vanessa, she was always calling me at work to bring home butterscotch ice cream and green olives."

"Tell me she didn't eat them together."

"She didn't. She ate the ice cream first, then followed with the olives. She had to have something sweet followed by something salty."

"Yuck."

"I thought it was a better combination than the chocolate and sardines she craved with Roxie."

Natalie groaned and put a hand to her mouth.

He laughed, then wrapped his arms around her for one moment of serious contact. "I promise you it'll be all right," he said, holding her tightly. "We'll find a solution that works for all of us, and you'll never be sorry you had this baby. All right?"

She held him as tightly as he held her. "Ben?" she asked.

"Yeah?" He waited for the words he wanted to hear.

What he got instead was, "I don't know. I can't seem to put the right words together."

"It's all right," he said, and kissed her cheek, then put her away from him. "You okay to pick up the girls?"

"Sure," she replied with a smile. "Everything as usual. See you at dinner."

He walked away, thinking there were only *three*

words and only one placement of them that made sense. How hard could it be?

But he'd promised himself he wouldn't force anything. He was just going to relax and accept that he was about to become a father again. He was a little surprised by how much that thrilled him.

Chapter Eleven

"We're going to have a baby." Vanessa repeated quietly what Ben had just told her and Roxie. It was the day before Thanksgiving.

Natalie combined three-quarters of a cup of applesauce with two cups of mincemeat and one and a half tablespoons of tapioca, afraid to look up. Greg Fortuna had confirmed her pregnancy that morning, and she was fighting mild nausea and major terror.

"How come?" Vanessa asked. The question wasn't belligerent, simply curious. "Natty's not your wife. She's just our friend."

Natalie felt Ben move to the counter where Vanessa stood beside her on the step stool, ready with a pie tin and a bottom crust.

"Now she's more than my friend," he said. "She's someone I care for very much."

Natalie had to admire that answer. She'd been wondering how they would explain the delicate service he'd provided. Since beloved children assumed all other children came from love, it was a wise reply.

"Oh." Vanessa seemed to find that acceptable.

"Is it a girl baby or a boy baby?" Roxie inquired.

She stood on a stool from the garage, ready to sprinkle cinnamon on the top crust.

"We don't know that yet." Ben touched her hair in a paternal, proprietary way that never failed to move Natalie. She remembered her father touching her that way only occasionally, not every day like Ben did with his daughters. "There's a test Natty can have a little later that'll tell us."

"I think we should have another girl!" Roxie said.

"Girls *are* better than boys," Vanessa agreed. "They don't spit and burp and stuff like that. Daddy, do you want a boy?"

"I'll take whatever we've got."

"What do you want, Natty?" Vanessa asked.

Relieved by their pleased reactions and the ease with which Ben had averted questions for which they had no answers, she smiled at her kitchen help. "I'd like another little girl just like the two of you."

That, too, seemed to be the right answer. Vanessa and Roxie beamed.

Ben gave her a congratulatory wink.

Lulu, however, was not as easy.

"I'm thankful the two of you have found each other," she said as Ben and Natalie helped her with Thanksgiving dinner, while the girls watched the Macy's Parade on television. "But I'm a little concerned about precisely *what* you've found in each other. If it's merely reproductive systems, I think you're selling yourselves and the entire concept of romance pitifully short. Natty, hand me the butter."

Natalie passed it across the chopping-block island,

noting absently that now even Lulu called her Natty. It made her feel included, despite Lulu's displeasure.

Lulu whipped butter into a pot of boiled potatoes, stopping occasionally to add cream.

Ben, putting olives, pickles and pearl onions in a divided dish, nudged Natalie surreptitiously with his elbow.

"I saw that," Lulu said without looking up from her mashed potatoes. "I know you're feeling like partners in crime, but partners in love would be far more productive."

"Please stop grumbling at Ben," Natalie said firmly, but politely. "I got him into it. It was all my idea. He didn't want to at first but..." She hesitated, wondering how to explain her mother.

"But?" Lulu prodded.

Natalie decided to lay it on the line. "But he heard my mother call me and berate me just like you're doing to him, and I guess he decided I needed an ally."

Lulu looked taken aback for a moment, then she said in a quieter voice, "I love all of you," she said, "and I'm just concerned about the way you've approached this. I mean, I know the cart often comes before the horse today, but it doesn't usually come without it altogether."

"We know what we're doing," Ben assured her.

Natalie looked up at him, knowing that her eyes asked clearly, *We do?*

He scolded her with a glance as he turned a bottle of green olives into the last segment of the plate.

"So, I'm just supposed to trust that when this child

is born, I'll have a grandbaby I'll be able to see occasionally?''

"You're just supposed to trust *me*," Ben said, carrying the plate to the table.

"Do you?" Lulu asked Natalie.

Natalie realized in some surprise that she didn't even have to think about it. "Implicitly," she said.

Dinner was a feast with the traditional turkey, all the trimmings and a few nontraditional favorites the girls had requested—macaroni and cheese, calico corn with sweet red pepper in it, and the Jell-O and fruit dish they'd told Natalie about.

Natalie ate until she was stuffed, horrified by how much she was able to consume.

"You're eating for two," Lulu said philosophically when Natalie groaned at her empty plate. "When I was carrying Ben, I once ate an entire carton of strawberry ripple ice cream in one sitting—and we're not talking the little gourmet pints we have today. We're talking the good old-fashioned half-gallon brick."

Natalie took some comfort in Lulu's svelte figure. "You've apparently been more careful since then."

She waved her fork at the stairs. "I'm always running up and down steps for one reason or another, and my friends and I have an in-line skating club. We call ourselves Widows on Wheels."

"How's Mrs. Baldwin?" Ben asked casually, pretending interest in a turkey wing while winking at the girls when Lulu was distracted with a second helping of dressing.

"She's fine, thank you for asking." The tone of

her reply suggested she knew his interest wasn't as noble as he'd made it sound.

"May we be excused," Vanessa asked politely, "so Roxie and I can collect leaves for my project? I still need a maple and a mountain ash."

"Okay," Ben replied. "Grandma's got both of those, so stay in the yard."

The girls raced for the back door.

"Put on your coats!" Natalie called after them. The weather had taken a definite turn from chilly to cold, and she'd been reminding them all week that they couldn't go outdoors in their sweatshirts anymore.

They hurried back to comply, then ran for the door again, slamming it closed before she could caution them not to.

She winced at the sound, then looked at Ben to find him studying her with an expression she couldn't quite interpret, except to see that he was amused by something.

She had a feeling it was her, though she couldn't imagine why.

"Joke?" she asked.

He raised an eyebrow innocently. "No," he said.

"It's because of all I ate, isn't it?"

"Not at all. I kept up with you admirably. Even surpassed you."

"Then what are you smiling about?"

"I'm anticipating mince pie for dessert," he said. When his mother would have stood, he put a hand on her arm to keep her in her chair. "I'll clear the table, you two relax. Anybody for more coffee?"

The reply was unanimous. He carried a stack of plates to the kitchen and returned with the coffeepot.

"You trained him to be so useful," Natalie praised Lulu.

"I did," Lulu agreed, splashing milk into her cup. "I knew it would make him more marriageable, and I was anxious for some other woman to worry about him for a change."

He carried off a small stack of dishes in his free hand, frowning over his shoulder at the discussion going on about him.

"Did you really worry about him?" Natalie asked when he'd disappeared.

Lulu sipped at her coffee, then leaned back in her chair. "Of course I did. He's the kind of man who'll be a friend to the end and love a woman with every breath in his body. People always take advantage of that kind of man."

Natalie didn't know if the courteous thing was to let the remark pass or confront it. Though she hadn't known Lulu very long, she'd observed that Ben's mother didn't appreciate subtlety.

"And you think I've done that?" she asked. "Taken advantage of him?"

"Not yet, perhaps," Lulu answered, seeming a little surprised that Natalie had chosen to deal with her in a straightforward manner. "But I'm wondering if a hard worker like him with two little girls is going to keep a celebrity like yourself in Dancer's Beach, Oregon, once you have what you want."

Natalie understood her concern and appreciated how the situation looked to her. "I have what I want right now, Lulu," she pointed out quietly. "If I was that kind of woman, I'd be gone already."

Lulu looked her in the eye. "I know the two of you agreed that if you were pregnant, you'd stay until the baby was born."

"I did. But he'd never make me stay if I decided to go. You know that. Nothing holds me here but my word and my respect for him."

Lulu wavered. "He's falling in love with you," she said aggressively.

Natalie waved a helpless hand. "I'm falling in love with him!"

Lulu closed her eyes, then opened them and shook her head. "Then why am I not hearing wedding bells?"

Natalie was getting tired of explaining this, because she seemed to have trouble grasping it herself. "Because I'm afraid of being a mother."

Lulu offered the predictable argument. "But you asked Ben to get you pregnant. That'll make you a mother."

Natalie frowned at her for underlining the obvious. "But that'll be a baby. Vanessa and Roxie are two lively little girls who'll need help and direction, and who once had a mother who was quite wonderful. Now all they'd have is me, who doesn't know the first thing—"

"Natty! Natty, look what we found!" Vanessa burst through the back door, followed by Roxie. They had fists full of maple and mountain ash leaves. "Wait till you see this really big one!"

Vanessa went to put the damp and dirty pile in the

middle of the table, but Natalie stopped her and opened out a page of the newspaper on the carpet.

"Let's look at them over here," she said, drawing the girls down to her, expelling a relieved breath over the near miss on Lulu's white lace tablecloth.

She glanced at Lulu, sharing a grin with her over the girls' excitement, then saw the same look in her eye that she'd seen in Ben's.

But the girls were pressing leaves into her hands and she didn't have time to think about it.

They had dessert and coffee and milk in the living room, the adults on the sofa, the girls sitting on the floor in front of the coffee table.

"This mince pie," Ben raved for the fourth time, "is incredible, Nat. This could be our fortune. Instead of Mrs. Fields cookies, we could open Mrs...." He hesitated, obviously not sure where to go with his remark.

"Mrs. Griffin's Pies," Vanessa filled in for him, having no such compunction. "But you'd have to get married for that. Or have Miss...what's your other name?"

"Uh, Browning," Natalie replied.

Vanessa shrugged. "That doesn't sound as good."

Vanessa went back to her pie, apparently satisfied that she'd made a sufficient contribution to the conversation.

Natalie forked another bite of pumpkin pie into her mouth and pretended not to notice Ben's hesitation or Vanessa's solution.

After dessert Vanessa commandeered everyone,

making them pass inspection on her leaves and select the ones for her school project.

She was fascinated by a red leaf about six inches across. It was perfect.

Ben held up a slightly larger one that was mostly red, but gold on the tips. "It's not quite as perfect as that one," he said, "but I like the gold color on the edges of this one and I think the dry spots make it kind of interesting."

"That's called the apex," Vanessa corrected didactically, pointing to the tips. "The bigger part is the lobe."

Ben dipped his head in apology. "Thank you for straightening me out."

"I like the perfect one!" Roxie chimed in, leaning over Ben to point to it. Then, unable, to get close enough, she climbed into his lap to study it.

"We're supposed to find them as perfect as possible," Vanessa said. "Don't you think the all-red one is prettier, Natty?"

Natalie took the leaf from Ben and studied it. "I think your dad means that this one's more real. There are very few really perfect things, and this one looks like it did its best to get big...." She touched the imperfections. "It got a few bumps along the way, but it's still here for us and really beautiful."

Vanessa thought that over, then firmly chose the red one. She handed the other to Ben. "You can have this one, Daddy."

"Thank you," he said.

They went home with bags of leftovers, but before

they left, Natalie earned a hug from Lulu for her grapevine wreath.

"I don't mean to interfere," she said for Natalie's ear only. "I just don't want to see any of you get hurt."

Natalie hugged her back. "I understand that, Lulu. I promise the last thing I'd ever do is deliberately hurt Ben or the girls."

"I guess that's all I can ask." Lulu freed Natalie, kissed each of the girls and blew a kiss to Ben, who was already in the van.

The girls went right to bed without complaint, replete with good memories and good food.

"It was a really great day," Vanessa said as Natalie hugged her while Ben tucked in her feet. "It felt like, um, sort of..." She made a circle of her hands.

"Like a balloon?" Natalie asked.

"No." Vanessa shook her head and yawned. "Just like a big round thing." She made the gesture again with her hands.

Mystified, Natalie watched Ben hug Vanessa and turn off her light. They walked together into the hallway.

"What did she mean?" Natalie asked.

He smiled as they stopped and faced each other in the hallway. "Sometimes her thoughts outdistance her ability to express them. I think she meant..." He made the circle with his hands. "Whole. Complete. Family. She had just turned six when Julie died, and it could be that she remembers that more as a feeling of wholeness that's been missing in our lives since then."

Wholeness. Natalie thought about that circle and wondered how she could ever be considered responsible for *completeness*.

Roxie was already asleep, the blanket pulled up over her head.

Natalie pulled it down to her chin while Ben tucked her in.

"I'm always afraid she's going to get carbon dioxide poisoning, the way she burrows under the blankets," Natalie whispered.

Ben laughed. "I know. She's like a little gopher."

He turned off her light and they went back downstairs.

"I'll build a fire," Ben bargained, smiling at her over his shoulder as he reached for the wood box near the fireplace. "If you'll put on the coffee and serve up another piece of mince pie à la mode."

She blinked at him. "Ben, you had two at your mother's. You're going to be sick."

He smiled winningly. "I've got room for another one. It's the best thing I've had in ages."

Natalie wandered off to the kitchen, flattered by his praise, warmed by the wonderful day, intrigued and a little alarmed by Vanessa's circle in the air.

As she ground coffee and sliced pie, she heard Ben at work in the living room, whistling. She reached overhead for a plate and stopped stock-still as she felt it—wholeness. Completeness.

A circle that enclosed her and the baby, and Ben and the girls.

"Oh, my God!" she whispered to herself.

MARIANNE BEASLEY DIDN'T like her; Natalie had been aware of that fact the first time she'd picked up Roxie at the day care center. The woman was flawlessly polite but without any real warmth, and she would always ask about Ben.

Natalie remembered what Ben had said about her, and tried always to be courteous in return. She hadn't understood men, either, until she'd met Ben.

"Would you ask him when he's coming by to give me that estimate?" Marianne asked Natalie as Roxie climbed into the car. "I'm anxious to talk to him about it."

"Of course I will," Natalie promised, and reached in to check Roxie's seat belt. Then she slid the side door closed.

Marianne was still there, watching her with a look that seemed to combine resentment, suspicion and confusion. "I expected you to be snooty," she said baldly.

Natalie nodded with a smile. "Everybody thinks that people on television or in the news are somehow different. We're not."

Marianne unbent just a little. "You're very pretty," she said.

"So are you," Natalie returned. "And without makeup. I look anemic if I don't have on foundation, blush and mascara. My eyelashes are white."

Marianne seemed to think she was being patronized. "I don't believe that for a minute. Don't forget to ask him about the estimate."

"I won't."

Natalie stopped for groceries on the way home, and

the usual late-afternoon routine left her complacently unaware of what would happen next.

She had potatoes on to boil, chicken breasts in the oven, and was chopping broccoli when a bloodcurdling scream came from somewhere upstairs. She froze.

Vanessa, working on her leaf collection at the kitchen table, looked up.

Then there was a thump and a loud shriek.

Natalie headed for the stairs, Vanessa right behind her.

"Roxie?" Natalie shouted when she looked into the child's room and found it empty. "Roxie!" She stopped to listen and heard wailing coming from Ben's room.

She followed it through the room and into the bathroom, where Roxie lay sobbing, a small puddle of blood on the floor beside her ear. The garage stool that had apparently been in front of the sink was toppled over.

Natalie knelt beside Roxie, her heart pounding. Her first thought was that Roxie must have fallen terribly hard for blood to be running from her ear. In a panicky flash she wondered how she would explain this to Ben.

Then she saw the needle protruding from Roxie's earlobe. The tiny lobe had been torn and the needle dangled awkwardly, drops of blood dripping onto the pristine white tile.

"Roxie!" she gasped. "What...?" Then Natalie realized what Roxie had been doing—piercing her ears herself!

She pointed Vanessa to the sink. "Vannie, wet a clean washcloth with cold water."

Vanessa hurried to comply and handed it to her.

Natalie put the cold cloth to Roxie's ear, fighting off the child's interfering hands. She pulled the needle free.

Roxie screeched as Natalie picked her up in her arms and hurried downstairs with her.

"Vannie, turn off the stove and the oven," she ordered, putting the screaming Roxie on her hip and reaching to the sofa for her purse.

Vanessa did as she asked.

"Can you get the door?"

Vanessa did that, too. Natalie handed her the car keys and Vanessa opened the SUV's door as she hurried out with Roxie.

Natalie knew putting a child in the front seat was not a good idea, but she wanted her in sight until she got to the clinic.

Roxie continued to screech.

"It's all right," Natalie soothed, reaching out to touch the child's tangled hair as she drove. "You're going to be all right. Blood is scary, but it's just a little bit."

"Paloma said it doesn't hurt!" Roxie wept. "But it hurts a lot!"

"You're not supposed to do it yourself, you silly!" Vanessa scolded. Then she looked at Natalie. "Roxie told me Paloma's big sister was at the day care today, and she has three holes in each ear. Roxie was mad because Daddy won't even let her have one."

Roxie sobbed on, huddled into herself, obviously feeling thwarted and abused.

Dr. Fortuna was sympathetic to Roxie *and* to Natalie. "Come on in," he said. "We can have that fixed up in no time." He carried Roxie into the examining room, adding in a smiling aside to Natalie, "I'm considering discount rates for families who bring me a patient once a week."

Roxie screamed mightily and had to be held down while Greg injected her ear with an anesthetic. Which struck Natalie as strange, considering the little girl had just stuck a needle in her own ear.

She quieted in a moment and lay still as the doctor stitched her ear.

Natalie took that moment to call Ben. She reached his answering machine and, unwilling to leave a message for fear he'd worry unnecessarily, she thought quickly. "Ah...would you bring home a pizza, please?" She asked.

"Bacon and pineapple," Roxie said pitifully from the table.

"Half bacon and pineapple," Natalie said, "and half whatever you and Vanessa like. Thanks. I just got...a little waylaid with dinner. Bye."

The doctor smiled at her as he bandaged Roxie's ear. "Good as new. I'll send you home with antibiotics. Come back in a week and we'll see how we're doing."

Natalie lifted Roxie off the table, accepted the prescription slip, collected Vanessa from the waiting room and set off for the pharmacy. She pulled into the driveway of the house right behind Ben.

He climbed out of the van, smiling as he came toward the car. A pizza box rested on the flat of his hand.

"Daddy!" Vanessa scrambled out of the car to meet him. "Roxie ripped her ear open and Natty pulled the needle out and drove really fast to the doctor's!"

Ben's smile turned to a worried frown as he put the pizza on top of the car and reached inside for Roxie.

"Hi, Daddy," she said, looking more like herself as he studied her ear. "I got four stitches and two shots and a Tootsie Pop!" She held it up proudly.

Natalie interpreted Vanessa's explanation as they walked into the house. Then she ran back to get the pizza off the roof of the van.

"She was just like Mom," Vanessa was telling Ben as he sat on the kitchen sofa with Roxie. "She knew what to do. She pulled out the needle and we had to turn off the potatoes and the chicken and Roxie got to sit in the front so Natty could watch her."

"Can I have some pizza now?" Roxie asked hopefully.

"If you promise me," Ben said, looking a little frantic, "that you'll never stick a needle in your ear again."

Roxie nodded gravely. "I promise. Want me to pour the soda?"

"Yes," he said, still frowning. "Okay. Let Vannie help you."

Natalie sat beside him, half expecting him to be

angry that she hadn't been watching Roxie more closely.

"Thank you," he said, pulling her into his arms. "Are you okay? Those things are usually harder on the parent than the child."

She felt the circle tighten around her. He wasn't angry; he understood. He'd called her "the parent."

There was little point, she decided, in fighting this anymore.

She raised her head from his shoulder and smiled into his eyes. "What are you doing a week from Saturday?" she asked softly.

He thought. "Meeting with the architect who's remodeling the third floor. Why?"

She leaned an elbow on his shoulder and nuzzled his cheek. "You want to get married instead?"

BEN HAD FELT THIS WEIRD sense of disorientation once before, when she'd asked him to give her a baby. And here he was again, afraid he'd misheard her, praying that he hadn't.

"To you?" he asked, thinking he'd better make sure she wasn't trying to plan his life before trying to take off on him.

Her lightly arched eyebrows came down in a threatening vee. "Is there someone else you'd rather be married to?"

His heart rate was picking up. "No, but I thought I'd better be sure what we're talking about. Seems to me you were dead set against it."

"That was before I realized I could deal with a mother crisis and not panic or fold." She kissed his lips slowly, lingeringly. "And before I realized how madly, deeply, desperately I love and need you."

He now felt it was safe to smile. In fact, he barely withheld a shout of laughter. "I guess I could move the architect to the afternoon," he said.

She giggled. "I might have other plans for you that afternoon."

"I'll move him to the following week," he said, "on the chance that it takes more than an afternoon."

She looped her arms around his neck and leaned into him with a contented little sigh. "I can't believe you happened to me, Ben," she whispered. "You, the girls, the baby. I've felt so alone and now... everything." She said it again, as though she still didn't believe it. "Everything."

He kissed her soundly, ardently, feeling a vague disbelief himself.

"What's going on?" a forceful little voice asked.

"They're kissing," another small voice replied.

"I *know* that, but how come?"

Ben and Natalie drew apart to find Vanessa and Roxie staring at them, Vanessa puzzled, Roxie watchful.

"Because we're getting married," Ben replied, reaching out to draw the girls between them. "What do you think?"

Vanessa smiled brightly. "I think it's cool." Then she added with sudden concern, "We aren't going to have to move, are we?"

Ben hadn't thought of that. He should have, but he hadn't. Natalie had a contract and commit—

"No," Natalie replied for him. "We'll just stay

right here and do what we've been doing since I came. Maybe I'll get a part-time job, but mostly, things will stay the same.'' She turned to Ben. ''Right?''

''Yes, right,'' he answered, privately reserving the right to think that might be difficult to pull off. But he didn't want to worry about it this minute. ''Roxie? Is that okay with you?''

''Yeah,'' she replied, as though she'd long ago accepted that Natalie was part of their lives. ''Can we have the pizza now? We set the table.''

''Sure.'' Ben stood and Natalie rose up beside him, sharing a smile over the casual way the news had been taken.

''One thing.'' Roxie stopped halfway to the table and turned to face Ben and Natalie.

Ben felt Natalie stiffen in concern beside him as he, too, worried about what was on Roxie's mind.

''Can you make French braids?'' the child asked.

''Yes,'' Natalie replied.

''Paloma has French braids. If I can't have the earrings, can I have the braids?''

Chapter Twelve

Dori screamed with delight when Natalie took Ben and the girls to meet her.

Sal, Dori's husband, came to the door with eight-month-old Max in his arms, to see why Dori was causing such a commotion.

"She's getting married!" Dori said, hugging Natalie again. "Sal, this is Natty's fiancé, Ben Griffin. Ben, my husband, Sal Dominguez."

Ben liked his direct gaze, his analytical once-over, his firm handshake.

The baby in his arms reached out for Ben. Ben took him, laughing, and the girls crowded closer, to Max's delight.

"We're going to have a baby!" Roxie announced to Dori and Sal.

"I heard that." Dori ushered the girls inside. "That's very exciting. Come on in and we'll see if we can find some cookies or cake. Don't trip over the toys."

The living room was a sea of toys. A large blanket was spread out in the middle of the room, and Ben placed the baby on it. The girls lay on their stomachs on either side of him and Vanessa gently pushed a ball toward him.

The baby laughed and, a rapport instantly established, slapped Vanessa on the head.

Sal smiled as he led Ben to the sofa. "I've taught him the refinements of dealing with women," he said.

Natalie and Dori went into the kitchen in earnest conversation.

"With the crop of women we're raising today," Ben said, pointing to his girls, "subtlety won't work. He may have to buff up his style a little, but he'll be way ahead of the other guys. Natty tells me you're in security."

"Yeah," Sal replied. "I have an office in Seattle. Dori came back into my life and I came here to help her with Max, so I'm moving my administration office to Dancer's Beach."

Natalie had told Ben that Max was simply left in Dori's car one day by a young unwed mother who admired Dori and wanted her to raise her son. How they'd come to this point in time was a long story.

"Women have a way of changing your life's direction," Sal said. Then, with a puzzled glance at Ben, he added, "You look familiar."

"You may have seen me at the Bijou Theater Building," Ben suggested, "if you ever do business there. I own it. I do all the maintenance and repairs myself, and I'm just getting ready to renovate the third floor into four upscale apartments. I'm there all the time."

Sal leaned forward interestedly. "We have friends

who have offices in your building. Athena Hartford's a lawyer, and Trevyn McGinty has a photo studio.''

Ben nodded. ''Fun tenants. When I first bought the building, I wondered about the wisdom of having to keep all those people happy, but I haven't regretted my decision for a moment. I'll have to talk to Trevyn about taking wedding photos.''

''So, you're a licensed carpenter?''

Ben nodded. ''And plumber, electrician, you name it. I used to build high-density housing in Portland.''

Sal leaned back with a laugh of pleased surprise. ''You're kidding! You're just the man I've been looking for.''

''Really.''

''I'm thinking of putting up homes in the woods on the hill outside of town.'' Sal smiled in self-deprecation. ''I do mostly bookwork now and I need a new project. I have a vague idea what I'm doing, but I've found in the past that a partner who really does know what he's doing is a valuable asset. Would you consider coming up there with me sometime when you're free and let me tell you what I have in mind?''

Ben nodded. ''I'd like to. Sometime after the wedding?''

''Good. Let me know. I'll pick you up. I want to start with a house for Dori and Max and me. Dori's brothers bought this place for a summer home, and they've been very generous in letting us stay here, but we can't impose upon them forever.''

Ben was happy at the prospect of a new project. Like Natalie and her kitchen and craft projects, he

loved to have something new underway. The third
floor of the Bijou was a new project, but the building
with all its old quirks and problems was not. Remodeling
was fulfilling, but not necessarily exciting.

His life was taking an amazing turn, he thought
with gratitude. A year ago, he'd wondered if he was
going to make it on his own. Now he, like Natalie,
had everything.

Dori came out of the kitchen with cups of coffee
and two glasses of milk on a tray, and Natalie followed
with a plate of cookies.

While they ate, Dori asked about Natalie's family.
"Your mother and brothers can stay here," she said.
"They are coming?"

Natalie sighed. "I haven't told my mother yet,"
she admitted. "She was horrified that I'd come to
Dancer's Beach to hide out, and when that story
showed up in *The Snitch,* she was mortified as well.
Wait until she hears that I'm staying here. And that
I'm pregnant."

Dori nodded sympathetically. "Well, she'd have
given you grief whatever you did, so I guess you just
have to bite the bullet and tell her."

"I know." Natalie sat up, brightening. "I was hoping
you'd stand up for me."

"Of course. I'd love to. How are you going to handle
invitations at this late date? I'm sure all the
McKeons will want to come."

"We'll call," Ben said, "since time's so short. My
mother's reserved the church's reception hall."

Those few details settled, they drank coffee and

shared cookies with the children, who gravitated toward the plate of sweets.

When they left, Ben gave Sal his business card.

Natalie asked about that on the way home, and Ben explained about Sal's business proposition.

"Wow," she said. "Did you know that you're considering going into business with a man who was formerly one of the foremost cat burglars in the world?"

Ben shot her a disbelieving glance. "What?"

"Yeah. He's Dori's sister-in-law's cousin. They were in the business as children because their fathers were."

"You're kidding!"

"No. It's a fascinating story. They're both on the up-and-up now, but you'll have to get him to tell you about it sometime."

"Who's her sister-in-law?"

"Julie McKeon. She's married to Dori's brother Duncan. You know, the actor?"

"Duncan McKeon," Ben said in disbelief as he pulled up to a light. "You're related to Duncan McKeon?"

"Yes."

He shook his head. "Amazing."

"You know what?" Roxie asked from the back seat.

Ben found her in the rearview mirror. "What, baby?"

"If we have a boy, it's okay, 'cause we really liked Max."

"Yeah," Vanessa added. "He's so cute. You don't think we could have a boy *and* a girl, do you?"

"You mean at the same time?"

"Yeah. Twins."

He grinned at Natalie's horrified expression. "No, I don't think so. There aren't any twins in our family. Are there in yours, Nat?"

She was about to deny that there were, then she remembered. "Actually," she said, "Duncan and Julie have twin girls."

He winced as the light changed. "But that's your cousin," he said, accelerating. "That's not a direct connection. Is it? I'm not sure how that works."

"Neither am I," she replied. "I think we should just plan on one," she said to the girls. "A really wonderful one. Okay?"

They agreed that it was.

GREG FORTUNA AGREED to be Ben's best man. "Happy to," he said. "But you could have fixed me up with a maid of honor who wasn't already married to someone else."

"Find your own woman," he said unsympathetically. They'd just repaired the inside banister at the men's mission and now sat in Burger's by the Sea, having steak sandwiches and coffee. "There are enough eligible women in town chasing after you."

"I don't have time for a social life," Greg said.

"I know for a fact that a relief doc comes in every other weekend."

"I have chores, errands...."

"And lots of excuses. Come on, Greg. You have time to volunteer for community service. Certainly you can work in one evening a week to try to meet women.''

Greg shook his head. ''I was married once. I didn't like it.''

Ben hadn't realized that. ''No kidding. What happened?''

''Incompatibility,'' Greg said simply, continuing to eat, apparently hoping Ben would drop the subject.

''She didn't like the doctor schedule?'' Ben persisted. It was true what they said about people in love, he thought. They wanted everyone else to fall in love, too.

''No, she was good about that,'' Greg said. He opened his mouth as though he might share more, then changed his mind. ''I moved here to put it behind me. Can we just say that it wasn't anybody's fault, but we ended up hating each other?''

''Sure. I'm sorry.''

''Not a problem.''

Ben grinned. ''I could give you a list of all the women who'll mourn when I'm out of circulation.''

Greg gave him a lethal glance as he slapped the bottom of the ketchup bottle he held over his french fries. ''They're all in preschool or on medicare. I'll just remain a happy bachelor, thank you very much.''

''You don't look happy.''

Greg put the ketchup bottle down and looked him in the eye. ''If you don't drop it, I know a group of underground organ harvesters who'd be happy to have your liver.''

Ben frowned. ''You don't *sound* happy, either.''

AFTER THE GIRLS HAD GONE to bed that night, Ben told Natalie about his exchange with Greg.

"We have to find him somebody," she said, coming toward the sofa where he sat, enjoying the fire blazing in the fireplace. "Dori must know someone."

"I suggested that, but he threatened to make me an organ donor without my consent."

"Ouch."

"That's what I thought." He reached for her hand.

She gave him her left, but kept her right hidden behind her back as she sat on one knee beside him, facing him.

"Close your eyes," she said.

He did it without hesitation.

She kissed him chastely, then took hold of his left hand, turned it palm up and placed something flat and cold in it.

"Okay, open," she said.

In his hand was a glass plate wrapped with a gauzy gold ribbon. But not any glass plate. He pulled off the ribbon and found a maple leaf in the glass, or so it appeared.

It was the leaf Vanessa had given him from her collection, the one she'd dismissed because it wasn't perfect, but that he'd liked for the same reason.

He turned over the plate and saw that a kind of rice paper held the leaf to the bottom of the plate, and some process made the paper seem to become part of the glass.

He turned the plate right side up again, the leaf clearly visible and somehow significant.

"It's wonderful, Natty," he said, pulling her to him for a kiss. "How did you do that?"

She shrugged, a little color tinging her cheeks. "I saw it on one of those craft shows. You just paint the leaf onto the plate with a special glue, then apply the paper and paint it on, and it all sort of magically becomes one. You can't put it in the dishwasher or anything, but you can wipe off the top. I thought you could eat your mince pie off of it."

She gave him a smile that seemed to come from deep inside her, and reached so far into him he could feel it in his bones. "I thought it was significant because that's probably the kind of wife and mother I'll be for a while," she said quietly. "I'll try hard to be great, but I know I'll have lots of worn and ratty places."

He put the plate on the cushion beside him and took her into his arms, his plans to watch the news and then catch up on paperwork disintegrating.

"You don't have any idea how happy you make us, do you?" he asked gently, holding her close. "You came into our lives like a candle at midnight. You stayed because you wanted something from me...." He put a hand to the soft curve of her belly, feeling the still-delicate roundness against his palm. "But I'm the one who got so much more in the bargain."

"I hope you still feel that way three months from now."

"I'll still feel that way," he promised, "forty years from now." He moved the plate to the coffee table, then tipped her backward onto the cushions. "I hope you didn't have any plans for this evening," he whispered, reaching for the zipper on her slacks.

"I did," she replied with a smile, putting her hands to his shoulders, "but yours seem compatible with mine."

HER MOTHER SOUNDED flabbergasted by Natalie's invitation to the wedding.

"What?" she gasped. "You're *marrying* him?"

"Yes," Natalie replied. Ben had sent her into his office to make the call so that she would have privacy. She decided that while her mother was shocked, she might as well tell her everything. "And, Mom, I'm pregnant."

There was an injured sound on the other end of the line.

"Ben and I made a deal," Natalie babbled, "because the sperm bank thing didn't work for me and I was so tired of dating and he...well, he didn't want to, then he changed his mind, and we took this trip...."

She knew she sounded like an idiot, but somehow, much to her own surprise, she wanted very much for her mother to understand. And she kept thinking that she had to have the right words somewhere, so if she just kept talking...

"He has two little girls, seven and five. They're adorable and very smart."

"That'll be *three* children, Natty, and you have absolutely no—"

"They're very happy about the wedding."

"What about your job? Your contract? You were

winning awards, gaining attention and additional airtime. Natty, you were on your way!''

"They're extending my leave, Mom. I don't think I'll want to go back, but if I do, they're giving me time."

"But to stop when you were just—"

"I'm happy here, Mom," she said firmly. "And Ben and the girls are happy about the baby."

"This is the 'entrepreneur.'" Her mother made the word sound like an epithet.

"Yes. He owns an historic building that has twenty shops and offices in it, and he's remodeling the third floor into apartments."

"A landlord." That, too, sounded like an insult.

Suddenly Natalie knew what would impress her and shamelessly trotted it out. "He's going into business with Sal Dominguez," she said. "You remember? Dori's husband?"

She knew her mother would remember. Sal had taken no guff from her on a visit Natalie and her mother had paid Dori this summer. He'd earned her grudging respect.

"I remember," her mother said, a spark of new interest in her voice.

"They're going to build a development on the hills outside of Dancer's Beach," Natalie added.

"Well." Letitia drew a breath, her voice softening. "I'm not convinced this is the best move you could have made, Natty, but if it means you're going to be happy and that you'll finally have what you want...then I guess all I can do is come to the wedding."

Natalie covered the mouthpiece and heaved a sigh of relief. As difficult as this had been, it was far easier than she'd imagined.

"Have you called your brothers?"

"I'm about to do that. I wanted you to know first."

"Very well. When shall I be there?"

They spent several moments discussing details, then her mother said goodbye and they hung up.

Natalie felt a sudden and rather violent wave of nausea and rushed to the bathroom.

Ben was there with a bracing arm and a cold washcloth.

"That bad, huh?" he asked.

"No," she replied weakly. "Not half as bad as I'd expected. I think I'm just getting into the barfing phase. This should really liven up the wedding."

"Want to try some dry crackers?"

"Do they really work?"

"They helped Julie."

Natalie leaned against his shoulder one more moment. "Then let's try it. She did everything else right."

"You'd have liked her," he said, helping her to her feet.

"I know. She's still very present here, and I *do* like her."

AFTER SCHOOL ON MONDAY, Dori drove Natalie, Vanessa and Roxie to town to shop for dresses for the wedding.

It was the first week in December and Christmas was everywhere they looked. Downtown Dancer's

Beach was strung with garlands and lights, and every shop window was decorated. White lights outlined the Bijou, the Buckley Arms, the library and city hall. A life-size manger scene stood on the church lawn, and Santa and his reindeer flew on cables above the trees in the park.

Barbara's Boutique in the Bijou Theater Building had everything for weddings, from nut cups to shoes for the wedding party.

Natalie hadn't formally established wedding colors, though she loved the deep claret-red dress Dori picked out. It had a round-necked velvet bodice, long snug sleeves and a long, full organza skirt.

"That's it," Natalie said. "We'll go with red and white. How perfect for the season."

Natalie thought her dark-haired cousin looked wonderful in the dress, but she knew the cost was considerable.

"I hate to have you spend a lot on something you might never wear again," she said.

Dori did another turn in front of the mirror. "I love it. And I'll wear it at Christmas. Sal and I are hosting the family for a few days, and this will really convince them that the baby of the family is finally a woman." She rolled her eyes at Natalie. "I thought the day would never come. Sal will love this dress. Now, what about the girls?"

Vanessa, enamored with Dori's dress, pleaded for a full-length style. Roxie seconded the plea.

Natalie, originally intent on something practical, soon abandoned that notion in the face of their excitement over being in the wedding.

After a long search, they finally found round-necked, puffy-sleeved dresses in a shade of dark pink silk that blended well with the claret. The girls twirled in front of the mirror, giggling happily.

Natalie was a little surprised to find such happiness herself in their delight.

Dori winked at her. "I have a feeling," she said softly, "that you're going to escape the wicked step-mother problems."

"I hope so." She put a hand to her stomach. "They feel as much my own as this one."

Dori hugged her. "I know what you mean."

The last duty of the day was the search for Natalie's dress.

Dori sat in a pink brocade barrel chair with the girls while the clerk helped Natalie in and out of several dresses. The fourth one she tried on made her draw in her breath.

"That's it," the clerk said reverently. "Let's go show your entourage."

It was white chiffon over a fitted silk slip with yards and yards of skirt. A simple round neck with a tiny collar swept into transparent diaphanous sleeves cuffed tightly at the wrist. And the whole was embroidered with a scattering of tiny white flowers.

The clerk walked her up a series of carpeted steps to a sort of dias in front of a three-way mirror.

"Oh, Natty!" Vanessa whispered, running to the bottom of the steps and stopping as though they were somehow sacred. "It's so pretty!"

"You look beautiful!" Roxie exclaimed.

Dori frowned at her in the mirror in pretended annoyance. "If your waist is twenty-two inches, I'm going to kill you."

"Yeah, right." Natalie made a scornful sound. "Relax. It's twenty-four and a half."

"That's it. You're dead."

Natalie considered that weirdly prophetic some moments later, after the clerk had checked the shoulders, the length of the sleeves, the fit of the waist and the length of the skirt, and finally declared the gown perfect.

Natty's companions claimed to be starving, and she started down the stairs to change out of the dress. The rubber soles of her tennies dragged on the plush carpet, stopped the momentum of her feet, though not her body, and she tumbled headlong down the stairs.

She had several panicky thoughts simultaneously.

The first was *The baby!*

The second, an attempt to be calm. *There are only six steps and they're carpeted.*

And finally, as she landed with a thud, first on her side, then her head, *Where did that table come from?*

She felt everyone crowding around her, heard shouts of "Natty!" and "Oh, my God!" Then there was a vicious wrench in her stomach and she fainted dead away.

BEN SANK INTO HIS favorite chair with a thermal cup of take-out chili from Burger's and turned on the football game. He seldom got to watch one without interruption, and as much as he loved the women in his life, he was looking forward to the quiet afforded him by the empty house.

They would have dinner after they shopped. He might get to see the whole game. He found the right channel, opened the side cup of cheese and onions and poured it over the steaming, aromatic mixture, then dipped his plastic fork into it.

The telephone rang.

Allowing himself a word he never used when Natalie and the girls were home, he hit the talk button and said querulously, "Hello!"

"Well, I don't really want to talk to you, either," his mother said, "but I was considering your wedding present and wondering whether to get you a wicker sofa and chair set like mine—you know, the one Natty admires every time you come here? Or if I should just give you a check toward a honeymoon whenever you can take it."

"Mom, that's very generous, but you don't have—"

"Which?" she asked, interrupting him.

He knew how much Natalie loved the wicker set, and it would be months before they'd be able to get away again.

"The wicker set, Mom. She'll love it."

"Well, don't tell her. I want it to be a surprise."

"Ha!" he teased. "You don't care if it's a surprise for me?"

"Your life's been filled with enough surprises. How are we doing on baby names?"

"The girls want Leia, if it's a girl, like Princess Leia in *Star Wars*. Natalie likes Margaret."

"Margaret." His mother mulled it over. While she did, he tried to figure out the score of the game. But not quickly enough. "Margaret. That's nice, simple. Preferable to those guy's names everyone's giving girls today. What are you doing tonight?"

"Eating chili and watching a football game." He said it without urgency.

"And I'm interrupting your bachelor night."

He smiled to himself. How many horrid, lonely nights after Julie died had been made bearable for him when his mom came over with a casserole, with a cake, with a shirt she'd found on sale and thought he should have?

"I love to talk to you when you're not nagging me about something," he said, grateful for her, but knowing she'd be embarrassed if he made too much of what he felt.

"Good. Then would you like to take this opportunity to thank me for asking you to take Natalie off my hands that night we couldn't wake her up and I'd promised her room?"

"Bless you for that, Mom," he said, temporarily giving up on the game. "I'm eternally in your debt."

"Then you'll take me in when I'm in my dotage instead of sending me to Geezer Hollow?"

He opened his mouth to form a teasing reply when there was a beep on the line indicating his call-waiting service.

"Hold on, Mom," he said. "I've got another call."

"No, that's all right," she said quickly. "I'll let you go. Talk to you tomorrow." She added hastily, "Love you."

"Love you, too," he replied, and she hung up.

He picked up the other call, giving up all hope of

ever seeing the game—or eating his chili while it was still hot. "Hello?"

"Ben, it's Dori." Her voice was high and tremulous.

He put the chili aside and sat up, dread coming to life in the pit of his stomach. "What is it?" he asked.

"Natty...um..."

No. This could not happen to him a second time. No!

"What?" he demanded, getting to his feet.

"She fell at the dress shop," Dori said in a rush. "I don't really know how bad it is, but she was out for a little while and Dr. Fortuna had the ambulance take her to Lincoln City. I tried to call you earlier..."

He found his keys and started for the back door. "Is the baby all right?"

"I don't know. The doctors are still with her. But that seemed to be...where her pain was."

"God."

"I know. Vanessa and Roxie are with me, here at the Lincoln City hospital."

"I'm on my way."

"All right," he told himself as he climbed into the van, screeched backward out of the driveway, then raced down the hill toward Highway 101. "I can deal with losing the baby, though it's a dirty, rotten trick. But I can't lose Natalie. I can't be stronger than death a second time. I can't."

The night was dark, the after-work traffic fairly heavy on the usually busy highway. He struggled to concentrate on driving, when his brain was really too beleaguered to think about anything but Natalie. And Julie.

He thought it was strange that Julie had been so safely tucked away in his memories since he'd fallen in love with Natalie that she'd come to mind only occasionally in the last few weeks. But now she was right there in the forefront of his mind, every feature clear, her smile bright—right beside the image of Natalie.

He blinked, but she was still there—bright, beautiful, the love of his youth, the mother of his children.

He pulled into the parking lot of the hospital without remembering the last few minutes of the drive. He ran to the desk and was directed to obstetrics.

He ran down the hall, feeling as though he was weighted down with an anvil. He'd gotten the same kind of phone call, remembered a similar high, tremulous voice telling him the woman he loved had collapsed, that an ambulance had taken her to Lincoln City. He'd run down the hall just like this, feeling the seams of his life ripping apart.

He stopped at the nurse's station, breathless with anguish. "Natalie Browning," he said.

"Oh, yes." A plump, middle-aged nurse smiled and got to her feet in what seemed like slow motion. She contributed to his feeling of being weighted down, slowed, stalled.

"Your family's in here." She opened a door into a pink-and-gray waiting area. He remembered this, too, from the last time.

Vanessa and Roxie flew into his arms. Roxie wept;

Vanessa looked desperate. He lifted Roxie and wrapped an arm around Vanessa.

"She isn't going to die, too, is she?" Vanessa asked. "Dr. Fortuna still hasn't come back."

Dori came to touch his arm. "No word yet," she said.

"How in the hell did she fall in a dress shop?" he demanded, his flood of anger carefully held in check.

"There were five or six steps," Dori replied with a helpless shrug. "She started down and the dress had a long, full skirt. I helped the ER nurse get her out of it when we arrived. She just fell. The steps were carpeted, the dais wasn't that high, but she sort of twisted, trying to save the baby, I think, and came down really hard against a decorative table at the side."

"Natty wouldn't talk to me!" Roxie sobbed, holding tightly to his neck.

Vanessa clutched his arm. "Can't we just take her home, like that other time she wouldn't wake up? Maybe if she could sleep with Starla..."

The door opened and Greg Fortuna peered into the room. He smiled briefly. "Ben," he said, beckoning.

Ben handed Roxie to Dori and kissed the top of Vanessa's head. "You guys stay with Dori and I'll be back as soon as I can to tell you what's happening."

"I want to come!" Roxie protested.

"We have to wait," Vanessa said, drawing her back.

In the hallway, Greg took Ben's arm and led him toward a pair of big double doors. "This was your lucky day, my friend,'' he said, giving him another smile. ''She has a few nasty bruises and she pulled a muscle. That's why she thought she had pain in her abdomen. But she's fine, and miraculously, so is the baby.''

Ben felt relief—he knew he did. His body just didn't seem to understand it. He followed Greg into an examining room, where Natalie lay on her back, her eyes closed, while another doctor watched a monitor to which she was attached.

Ben could see her breathing, hear her groggy answer to the doctor leaning over her, but his mind seemed to interpret the scene as something else.

In his mind's eye, his memories of that awful day with Julie seemed to slip right over what was happening with Natalie at this moment, like an overlay on a blueprint that altered the image underneath.

It had been his lucky day, Greg had just told him, but Ben's memories were reminding him that this was what it was like to love someone. The threat of harm, the possibility of loss, was always there.

It was painful and ugly to lose a wife, but it was a similar kind of hell to have survived that to fall in love again and know that, every day, he ran the risk of suffering that pain all over again.

Natalie turned her head to the side, spotted him and held her hand out to him with a weak smile. ''Hi,'' she said feebly.

He went to her and took her hand, weirdly unable to focus on what was happening. His brain persisted with the image of what *had* happened nineteen months ago.

"You look awful," she said.

"Thanks." He struggled to hear her, to concentrate on her. "I was settling in for a quiet night of football—"

She squeezed his hand. "Oh, they're all the same. First downs, touchdowns, forward across the field, backward. Who cares?"

Greg, looking over the shoulder of the doctor reading the monitor, gasped indignantly. "Natalie! The whole world cares."

"The female part doesn't."

Greg caught Ben's eye across the bed. "If you want to leave her overnight, there's a sports network sensitivity chip we can install in her brain...."

Ben didn't react to the joke and Greg stopped. Natalie looked at Ben in concern.

The doctor watching the monitor made some notes on a chart and excused himself, promising to be back in a few minutes. Greg followed him.

The moment the door closed behind them, Natalie sat up, wincing as she put a hand to her head.

"Are you supposed to sit up?" Ben asked, supporting her back in the thin hospital gown.

She opened pain-filled eyes and focused on him. "Ben, what's the matter?" she asked.

"You're bruised, and you pulled a—"

"I know what's wrong with me," she interrupted. "I want to know what's wrong with you."

"Nothing," he replied. "You just scared the hell out of me, that's all."

She studied his eyes, and he had the most uncomfortable feeling that she could read him, way down to the terror he was still having trouble dealing with despite Greg's assurances that she was fine.

"There's something else," she insisted.

"No," he said firmly. "There isn't."

Her lips and her jaw firmed, and her eyes grew wider. "*Is* the baby really all right, or are all of you just telling me that because you're afraid I'll—"

"The baby's fine," he assured her quickly, firmly. "I'd tell you if it wasn't."

"You're sure."

"I'm sure."

"Then why do you look as though you've just lost everything, when I'm...?" Something flashed in her eyes and she stopped and stared at him.

"It's Julie," she said in a sad whisper.

Chapter Thirteen

Natalie's headache suddenly paled in comparison to her grinding heartache. Ben wasn't over Julie; he'd just thought he was because Natalie was carrying his baby. The details of this day had probably brought it all back to him—the telephone call, the rush to the hospital.

He was startled by what he felt; she could see it in his eyes. He couldn't help himself. He would always love Julie.

He sighed, looking tortured, and put a tender hand to her back. "I'm so grateful that you're all right," he said. "And that the baby isn't hurt."

"I'll be fine," she said, surprised that she had the voice to speak when she felt as though air had stopped moving through her lungs. Her heart was beating, but painfully.

Still, she would be fine. She'd survived before; she would survive again. And this time she had a baby to love.

The door opened, Greg led Dori and the girls into the room, and suddenly Natalie's resolve disintegrated. She would not be fine at all. She'd come to love Ben's girls as though she'd given birth to them, and there was no standard against which to judge her love for Ben. The extent of it was astronomical, exponential.

But she chatted and smiled as Dori helped her into the pants and sweater she'd worn shopping; as Ben and Greg helped her into a wheelchair, as the examining obstetrician gave her a list of instructions for her care once she got home, as Dori gathered Natalie's purse and jacket and followed the little parade out to the van.

Dori gave Natalie a quick hug, then frowned a little as she looked into her eyes. "You going to be okay?"

"Sure."

She looked from Ben to Natalie. "Want me to keep the girls tonight?"

"No," Natalie said before Ben could reply. "Thanks. But I'm really fine." And she needed tonight with them. "I'll call you if we need you, though."

"You promise?"

"Hope to die," she said, then realized what an inappropriate reply that was. She glanced at Ben, but he hadn't noticed—or pretended he hadn't. He was busy getting the girls into the van.

"You're *sure* you're okay?" Dori whispered to Natalie while Ben was distracted.

"Absolutely sure. I'll call you tomorrow."

Ben helped Dori into her car, thanked her for all her help, then shook hands with Greg, who stood alone with the empty wheelchair.

"About my volume discount..." Greg began.

Ben punched him in the shoulder, then climbed into the van.

The girls rattled on excitedly as they drove home, repeating for Ben's benefit the details of the shopping expedition and Natalie's fall.

"We got the coolest dresses!" Vanessa said excitedly, her enthusiasm for being in the wedding renewed now that she knew Natalie was safe. She went on to describe the color of pink. "Roxie gets to wear her hair up with flowers in it. I get to wear a sort of crown thing."

"I want a crown, too!" Roxie insisted and life for the girls returned to normal.

When they finally went to bed, after a dinner of grilled cheese sandwiches and chicken noodle soup, it was clear that things between Ben and Natalie were not back to normal at all. Natalie was sitting on the kitchen sofa under a blanket, where she'd spent her first few days with Ben and the girls. But Ben kept moving about restlessly, the gentle ease in his manner completely gone. He was tense, curiously angry.

"Can you sit with me for a minute?" she asked, desperate for one small space of time that might recapture what her clumsy fall seemed to have obliterated.

He was returning from the living room with a cold bowl of chili, evidence of his aborted attempt to watch the football game.

He held up the bowl. "I was going to get the dishwasher going. Put some clothes in the—"

"Just for a minute," she pleaded.

He put the bowl down on the counter and came to

sit at the foot of the sofa, where he'd once gently rubbed her cold feet, then put woolly socks on them. He looked anything but comfortable.

"I'm going to simplify things for you," she said with an attempt at cheer, praying that the burning lump in her chest didn't rise into her throat and make her cry.

He studied her suspiciously. "What, specifically?"

"Your life," she replied. "I'm going to let you have it back."

She waited for some sign of relief, for an indication that he was grateful for her magnanimity.

But his expression remained suspicious, with an added element of hostility. "I wasn't aware you'd taken it away," he said.

She sighed, thinking this would be easier on both of them if he wouldn't be so obtuse. "You know what I mean. I blundered into it and changed things you never really wanted changed. So I think we should change it back. I'm leaving."

He was eerily still. The only thing that moved was his eyebrow as it arched. "No," he said quietly. "You're not."

"It's the only sensi—"

"We had a deal."

"Yes. And it was contingent on the premise that you were over Julie and ready to move on. But you're not."

He opened his mouth to argue and Natalie rushed on. "And I don't want to force you into doing that. She was wonderful and you loved her and I don't want to rip that away from you."

"Tonight was remembered grief," he said. "That was all. I love you."

"I know you do," she said, reaching to the back of the sofa where his hand rested. "But only in that I remind you of what you lost with her. But I understand."

"No, you don't," he said, coolly angry. "This is your convenient excuse to run off with the baby so you don't have to face all the challenges of loving a man who once loved someone else, and raising another woman's children. Figuring out if you can find satisfying work that doesn't involve the spotlight. You're making it easy for yourself, Nat, not easy for me."

If her head hadn't been banging so hard, she might have hit him. She suddenly felt the same hostility she saw in his eyes. Proof, she thought, that this relationship was over.

"We'll talk about this in the morning," he said, as though issuing an edict. "I'll take you upstairs."

He lifted her in his arms, carried her up to her room and deposited her gently on top of the covers.

She opened her mouth to offer another argument, but he shushed her. "The girls are asleep," he said, "and they've been through enough tonight without hearing us fight."

He wrapped an arm familiarly around her legs, lifted her hips off the coverlet and then drew it and the blankets out from under her and covered her with them.

"How do you feel?" he asked, adjusting the blankets at her feet.

"Angry," she replied, folding her arms atop the blanket, "disenfranchised and second class."

"And so you should," he replied brutally. "Only second-class people run away. I meant how do you feel physically?"

"Second...!" she began in indignation.

"Headache?" he interrupted mildly.

"Yes," she snapped. "A big one! About six feet two!"

He left the room and returned with the pain relievers the doctor said were safe to use during the first trimester.

She dutifully took them with a few sips from the glass of water he'd also brought, then lay back and closed her eyes, wondering what had happened to her plans for a dignified exit. "Good night," she said firmly.

He replied pleasantly. She heard the click of her light, his retreating footsteps, then nothing.

Nothing. In the space of several hours, she thought, emotion rushing out of her like water down a drain, she'd gone from having everything to having... nothing.

That wasn't true, she corrected gravely, running a hand over her stomach. But becoming pregnant had once been the single, most important goal in her life. She'd desperately needed a receptacle for all the love inside her.

Then Ben and his daughters had come into her life—or she'd come into theirs—and suddenly love hadn't been as much about having something of her very own as having something to share.

She would see that Ben shared this baby. She would get a lawyer the moment she got back to Philadelphia and set up an amicable agreement. Ben had claimed he could never be a long-distance father, but there seemed to be no other way to solve this dilemma.

She liked Julie, though she'd never met her, but she couldn't live with seeing her in Ben's eyes.

BEN PACED HIS OFFICE holding a shot of bourbon in a barrel glass. He was just beginning to get over the shock and the barbed memories Natalie's accident had brought back.

He'd thought he had the past under control, but the simple truth seemed to be that pain that deep defied control. It came back to cut the ground out from under you at the damnedest times. And for a while there, he'd felt lost in the old stuff of his life, trapped in old grief and memories.

But he was back on his feet again. Julie had slipped away. Not far, probably, but sufficiently that he had his bearings.

Natalie was his life now, the mother of his baby, the woman his daughters adored and who adored them. And, mercifully, she and the baby were safe.

He felt a little panicky when he remembered that look in her eyes when she'd guessed he was thinking of Julie. A light had gone out of them. She'd looked defeated.

If she'd never been in love before, she wasn't aware of the things love could survive. She wouldn't understand the sturdy, miraculous scope of it. He would explain that to her in the morning.

Meanwhile, he thought, downing the last of the bourbon, if he was going to be coherent at all in the morning, he'd have to get some sleep.

He turned the lights out and went to bed.

NATALIE SOBBED QUIETLY as she packed. It was 6:00 a.m. She put artwork the girls had given her in the bottom of her case, then packed her clothes atop it. She placed the watch cap Ben had bought her on their trip on the very top, and considered it a sign of great maturity and control that she didn't dissolve altogether.

Then she remembered the small pile of laundry she'd left in the bathroom hamper. Reclaiming it to stuff in a plastic bag to take along, she found the longies Ben had lent her.

Natalie dropped them back in the hamper and made it to her room before the maturity and control she'd just praised herself for deserted her altogether.

Finally deciding that crying wasn't going to help anything, she closed and locked her case, grabbed her jacket and tiptoed past the girls' rooms without looking in, knowing she wouldn't be able to stand it.

She ran lightly down the stairs and out to the SUV. She'd leave it in long-term parking at the airport and call Ben from Philadelphia to tell him where to find it.

She put the key in the ignition and, forcing herself not to take one last look at the house where she'd been so happy, she put the vehicle in reverse and backed out of the driveway as quietly as possible.

Once on the street, she hit the accelerator, needing to get away before anything could stop her.

BEN AWOKE TO THE SOUND of a motor. A familiar motor. It took only an instant for him to understand what was happening. With a muttered expletive he rolled off the bed and onto his feet. He went to the window and swiped the curtain aside just in time to see the SUV screeching down the hill.

He'd never catch her in the van, he thought with a sense of desperation, grabbing for his clothes. Then an insidious thought occurred to him. He picked up the phone.

NATALIE CONCENTRATED on planning her future to distract herself from bouts of sobbing. She had to get it together, she told herself firmly, or she was going to cause an accident.

Impatient drivers and big trucks sped past her on Highway 18, the road that ran from the coast inland, the fastest route to Portland. The map with which she'd navigated the drive from Portland to the coast she'd left in her rental car.

She'd find her way, she told herself bracingly. What she should think about was what she intended to do with her life.

She had enough savings to do nothing until the baby was born. For reasons she didn't understand and couldn't explain, she was no longer interested in her old job. It could be, she mused, that life in Dancer's

Beach had slowed her down, or that the big picture of the news seemed less relevant to the average person than she'd once thought. Important to know about, of course, but less relevant.

She'd have to sell her condo and buy a house. That should be priority one before the baby came. Something with a yard and trees and maybe a porch. Something like Ben's house. She sobbed for the next five minutes, then, deciding that was counterproductive, not to mention dangerous while she was driving, she let the thought go.

She would have to find another job. She toyed with the idea of proposing to the network her idea of a show featuring recipes, decorating and crafts for the average woman.

Ben and Lulu had loved her grapevine... She sobbed for another five minutes, wondering if she would ever have another thought or idea that wasn't somehow connected to the Griffins and Dancer's Beach.

A truck honked and sped around her, and she pulled herself together one more time. *God, this is going to be an interminable drive,* she thought, glancing in her rearview mirror to see if there was anyone else behind her.

That was when she saw the red, flashing lights of the police car. With a groan, she pulled over into the driveway of a truck stop.

The officer was about Ben's age, with bright red hair and dark blue eyes. He appeared kind but firm as he leaned down to look at her while she opened her window. His eyes went over her face, still wet with tears, and he asked politely, "Are you all right, ma'am?"

"No," she replied honestly, "but I'll live. What have I done, Officer..." She checked his badge. "Officer Stone?"

"May I see your license and registration, please?" he asked, ignoring her question.

Resignedly, she dug out her license and reached for the registration on the back of the sun visor.

"You're from Pennsylvania," he said, copying down some information off her license.

"That's right. I was visiting...friends. I'm on my way home."

"I see." He studied the registration. "And this would be your friend's car? It's registered to a Mr. Griffin."

"That's right."

"And you're taking his car home?"

"No, I..." She knew she looked guilty. Whenever she was suspected of guilt, her face immediately took on the appearance of a perpetrator. And she had borrowed Ben's car. "I'm leaving it at the airport."

"And he lent it to you for this purpose?" The officer's eyes were boring into hers, though the question was softly spoken. She bet he was brilliant in interrogation.

She'd come this far, she told herself. A lie would either help her get back on the road or stop her altogether. She had a fifty-fifty chance.

"Yes," she said finally. "He lent it to me."

"Then I wonder why he reported it stolen?" he asked in that same relaxed tone.

She closed her eyes, the urge to sob coming back with a vengeance. Considering what had happened to her in the last few months, why would she ever have gambled on a chance that was only fifty-fifty?

"Officer, look—" she began.

But he cut her off, saying, "Would you get out of the car, please, ma'am?"

"But I didn't *steal* it!" she insisted, leaning out of her window toward him in her urgency to make him understand. "I just borrowed it to go to the airport."

That sounded so lame she put a hand to her face in humiliation.

"Please, ma'am," he said again. "Out of the car."

She unlocked her door and pushed it open, tears of frustration spilling from her eyes. "I was going to fill the gas tank," she grumbled.

He opened the back door of his unit and gestured her into it.

She held her ground. "Are you *arresting* me?" she asked in disbelief.

"You're driving a stolen car, ma'am," he said reasonably.

"It's borrowed!" she repeated.

"Without the owner's permission," he pointed out.

"The owner and I," she tried to explain, "aren't...communicating very well."

He gestured again to the back of his car. "Have a seat, ma'am," he said, "and we'll sort this—"

Before he could finish, there was a screech of brakes, then the crunch of tires on the gravel behind them.

Natalie heard the sounds absently, more concerned

about her impending incarceration than reckless driving. Until she noticed the look of obvious relief on the officer's face and turned to see a familiar blue van pull up.

Ben leaped out and strode purposefully toward them, his face set in grim lines.

On one hand, she was exasperated that she hadn't escaped Oregon without having to explain her departure, but on the other, she was enormously relieved to see someone who could explain to Officer Stone that she wasn't a thief.

The words Ben and the officer exchanged next destroyed what little sense of balance she'd managed to maintain.

"Hey, Adam," Ben said with a nod in the officer's direction. "I owe you big."

"Damn right you do," Stone replied. "My badge is on the line if you two don't work this out and she turns vindictive."

"Don't worry about that," Ben assured him. "Thanks again."

"Sure." With a smiling tip of his hat to Natalie, Stone climbed into his car and was off.

Natalie was as close to murder as she'd ever felt. "Don't worry about it?!" she demanded, turning on Ben in a rage that she didn't seem able to control. "You have your friend arrest me for stealing a car you *gave* me, and you tell him not to worry about it?!"

"Serves you right," he said with no apparent remorse, "for claiming to love me and the girls, then running out on us without a word."

"I tried to explain it to you last night, but you wouldn't listen. You wouldn't even let me talk."

"Because you were talking foolishness."

"I was trying to be honest," she said, her temper caving in on itself. She tossed her head, fighting the rush of tears again, holding them back through sheer force of will. "And I was trying to make you see the truth."

"Oh, I see the truth," he countered. "You want it all your way. From the very beginning, this was all about what you had to have to make your life complete. It didn't matter what it took, whose peace of mind was at risk, as long as you got it."

She bristled anew. "You agreed...!" she began hotly.

"And so did you." He pointed a finger at her. "In fact, *you* proposed to *me*. What's this?" He gestured toward the truck stop. "Separate vacations already?"

"This is me," she said, her throat closing and making speech difficult, "trying to give you what you seem to need."

"No, it isn't." When she turned away from him at that, he caught her arm and held her in place. "How can you give me what I need if you don't ask me what that is? All you *ever* do is tell me what you need, or tell me what *you* think I need."

"Don't yell at me!" she screamed at him.

"Then how in the hell do I get your attention?" he shouted back.

BEN FREED HER ARM and took several paces away from her, concentrating on drawing deep breaths. One more minute and he was going to swing her over his shoulder like a rolled up carpet and put her in the van.

But though muscle would work for the moment, it wouldn't for the long term. He had to figure out how to get through to her that he loved and needed her.

He turned back to her, saw that she looked as wild as he felt, and took that for a good sign.

He drew another breath and prayed for the right words.

"I'm sorry," he said, "if you thought I was thinking of Julie yesterday and not of you. My concern was for you, but the way it happened brought back memories of that other day. We all loved Julie, but she's gone. We accept that."

"I think you want to," she said, her voice high and tight, "but I don't think you have."

"No," he said firmly, his voice rising despite his best efforts at remaining calm. He simply couldn't be calm about her leaving. "You're the one who hasn't accepted it. You went shopping for a father for your baby as though you could find the perfect combination of qualities to make the perfect human being. Well, you're the broadcaster, but Natty, *I've* got news for *you.* No one's perfect, not even you. And you happened to pick a father for your baby who once loved another woman and already has two beautiful children."

He stopped and drew a breath, ran a hand over his face, then shifted his weight and met and held her gaze. "I know you wanted this baby because you wanted something that would be exclusively yours.

And, I'm sure, like a lot of lovers, you probably wish our relationship was pure and pristine, that this was first love for both of us. But then, what happens to those of us who are a little hard-used, who have old baggage and old pain? Are we out of the running?''

She raised tearful eyes to him, her expression half glowing, half fiercely protective. ''Your children would never be a problem for me. I love them, too!''

''Then loosen up,'' he pleaded, ''and love me. I can't help it that Julie was in my life before you. She'll always be part of who I am, but I'm ready to go on. Are you coming with me?''

He held his breath. This wasn't a move for the faint-hearted.

Natalie burst into hysterical sobs.

Great. He'd sent her over the edge. She was probably nauseous, exhausted and emotionally upset. He was considering his options when she threw her arms around him. ''I'm sorry!'' she said as she wept. ''I really wanted to do what was right for you. What do you want? I'm sorry I never asked. Please tell me what you want.''

He held her close and replied as clearly and as plainly as he knew how. ''I want you,'' he said. ''You and our baby with Van and Roxie and me. That's all. That's everything.''

''Okay.'' She raised her head to look into his face, her eyes reflecting happiness for the first time since he'd seen her in the emergency room last night. ''That's everything for me, too.''

''Then the wedding's still on for Saturday?''

''Yes.'' She hugged him again, then teased him

with a frown. "But wait until I get hold of Officer Stone."

Ben laughed, feeling as though a truck had been lifted off his chest. "He's invited."

NATALIE SUDDENLY BECAME aware of an audience of four standing behind Ben, their expressions cautiously hopeful. There was Vanessa, Roxie, Lulu and...her mother!

Natalie gasped, a hand to her heart.

Her mother crossed the small distance between them and offered her a strong but quick hug.

Natalie wanted to hold on, but she knew better. This was the best her mother could do. She'd come to the wedding. That was all Natty could ask.

"Mom, you're early. I thought you couldn't get away until Friday."

"Lulu called and encouraged me to come earlier," Letitia replied. "She's going to put me up until the wedding, and we're going to get acquainted. Your brothers are coming on Friday."

Natalie looked from one to the other in amazement. It was a little like the meeting of two goddesses, thankfully allied rather than at odds. She was certain they could generate thunder if they chose.

"But, how did you all end up here?" Natalie looked at her watch. "It isn't even eight o'clock yet."

The girls ran forward. Natalie leaned over them and gathered them into her arms.

"I woke up as you left," Ben explained with a roll of his eyes, "and knew I couldn't catch you, so I called Adam on his cell phone."

"Officer Stone."

"Yes."

"But won't you be in trouble for making a false accusation, or something?"

"No. Adam said he'd log it as an ATL, an attempt to locate. They're pretty informal, but he did go a little above and beyond, getting you out of the car and making you wait until I could get here."

"Vannie heard the car, too!" Roxie reported. "And she asked Daddy if we could come!"

"I intended to drop them at Mom's," Ben added, "but she was coming out of the house with your mother when I pulled in. So, of course, when they heard you'd taken off, they had to come along, too."

"We were on our way to surprise you!" Letitia said. "We even have a coffee cake in the van."

Lulu reached over the girls to give Natalie a hug. "I picked her up at the airport last night. I hope you don't mind. I wanted her to know how lucky I feel that we have you."

"Thank you, Lulu." Natalie hugged her again.

"All right!" Ben gathered everyone up. "Let's go home, where we belong."

"Want me to drive the van?" Lulu offered. "So you and Natalie can drive back in the SUV and, you know, work on your communications skills?"

Ben handed her his keys.

"I'm going with them," Natalie said, pretending to head for the van. "They have the coffee cake."

Ben swept her up in his arms and carried her to the SUV. "Too bad Henrietta Caldwell isn't here," he teased, "to get a photo of this for *The Snitch*."

Natalie hugged him and laughed. "I wouldn't even care. I'm kind of getting into our being notorious."

Behind them, the girls squealed delightedly as they skipped back to the van, each with a grandmother by the hand.

Roxie had Letitia, Natalie noticed as Ben set her on her feet to open the car door. Betsy was dangling from the child's other hand and, as she held the doll up, Letitia dutifully admired it. Roxie was squinting up at her and talking a mile a minute.

Letitia nodded, then tipped her head back and laughed at something Roxie said.

"This will be good for her," Natalie said.

BEN TURNED NATALIE'S FACE toward him and kissed her. "This will be good for me, and I promise you it'll be good for you."

Natalie wrapped her arms around his neck and smiled with a joy that seemed to come from deep inside.

"It's already been good for me," she whispered. And just before she reached up to kiss him back, he saw stars in her eyes.

Epilogue

Leia Margaret Griffin was born at 3:27 a.m. on August 10. She was very bald and very cranky.

"Oh, boy," Natalie said as she lay propped up against Ben's chest in her hospital bed later that morning, his arms wrapped around both of them. Vanessa and Roxie crowded in on either side. "She's not very happy with us."

"When she comes home," Roxie said, "we'll let her sleep with Starla. That'll make her happy."

"What color do you think her hair will be?" Vanessa asked, touching a tiny hand. "She doesn't even have one piece!"

"We'll just have to wait and see," Ben replied.

Roxie held up one of her French braids which Natalie had made at home just before her labor started. "Mom won't be able to make these for her for a long time."

Vanessa ran a hand over her own hair, now almost to her chin after nine months of letting it grow. Natalie had bought her fancy barrettes.

"I wanted short hair at camp," Vanessa had explained to her and Ben when they'd been shopping.

Ben had a skipping Roxie by the hand, but Natalie remembered him turning to listen to his oldest daughter's explanation. "Because all the girls there had moms who came to visit, and their moms would brush their hair, or play with it while they talked to them, or brush it out of their faces. And I didn't have a mom, so I didn't want the hair."

She'd tucked her arm in Natalie's and leaned her head against it as they stopped at a rack of hair accessories. "But now I have a mom, so I want my hair back."

Ben had looked as touched as Natty had felt. Then he'd winked at her.

That was the moment when she'd felt she had truly been absorbed into the family. And there'd been moments since when she'd almost forgotten that she hadn't given birth to Vanessa and Roxie.

There was a knock at the door, then Lulu peered around it. She came to the bed to give Natalie a hug.

"That's from your mother," she said. "She just called and said to tell you that the most fabulous musical teddy bear is on its way by FedEx."

Lulu and Letitia had become fast friends, and Letitia had turned into a doting grandmother who sent things to Vanessa and Roxie all the time.

"And I think there are some things in the package for you two, also." She drew the girls gently off the bed, then leaned over to touch the baby's head. "Bye, little one. We'll be there to welcome you home tomorrow." She straightened, then hugged Natalie once more. "This hug's from me. I'll take the girls home with me. Let us know what time you'll be home and we'll have everything ready."

She hugged Ben, the girls said their goodbyes, and Ben, Natalie and Leia were alone.

Natalie leaned back against Ben and let herself feel the wonder of the helpless baby in her arms, and the strong, protective man behind her who held her in his. She was sandwiched in between all the world had to offer.

She truly did have everything.

Harlequin truly does make any time special. ... This year we are celebrating weddings in style!

A Walk Down the Aisle
WEDDING CELEBRATION

To help us celebrate, we want you to tell us how wearing the Harlequin wedding gown will make your wedding day special. As the grand prize, Harlequin will offer one lucky bride the chance to **"Walk Down the Aisle"** in the **Harlequin wedding gown!**

There's more...

For her honeymoon, she and her groom will spend five nights at the **Hyatt Regency Maui.** As part of this five-night honeymoon at the hotel renowned for its romantic attractions, the couple will enjoy a candlelit dinner for two in Swan Court, a sunset sail on the hotel's catamaran, and duet spa treatments.

A HYATT RESORT AND SPA

Maui • Molokai • Lanai

To enter, please write, in, 250 words or less, how wearing the Harlequin wedding gown will make your wedding day special. The entry will be judged based on its emotionally compelling nature, its originality and creativity, and its sincerity. This contest is open to Canadian and U.S. residents only and to those who are 18 years of age and older. There is no purchase necessary to enter. Void where prohibited. See further contest rules attached. Please send your entry to:

Walk Down the Aisle Contest

In Canada	In U.S.A.
P.O. Box 637	P.O. Box 9076
Fort Erie, Ontario	3010 Walden Ave.
L2A 5X3	Buffalo, NY 14269-9076

You can also enter by visiting www.eHarlequin.com
Win the Harlequin wedding gown and the vacation of a lifetime!
The deadline for entries is October 1, 2001.

HARLEQUIN®
Makes any time special ®

HARLEQUIN WALK DOWN THE AISLE TO MAUI CONTEST 1197
OFFICIAL RULES
NO PURCHASE NECESSARY TO ENTER

1. To enter, follow directions published in the offer to which you are responding. Contest begins April 2, 2001, and ends on October 1, 2001. Method of entry may vary. Mailed entries must be postmarked by October 1, 2001, and received by October 8, 2001.

2. Contest entry may be, at times, presented via the Internet, but will be restricted solely to residents of certain georgraphic areas that are disclosed on the Web site. To enter via the Internet, if permissible, access the Harlequin Web site (www.eHarlequin.com) and follow the directions displayed online. Online entries must be received by 11:59 p.m. E.S.T. on October 1, 2001.

   In lieu of submitting an entry online, enter by mail by hand-printing (or typing) on an 8½" x 11" plain piece of paper, your name, address (including zip code), Contest number/name and in 250 words or fewer, why winning a Harlequin wedding dress would make your wedding day special. Mail via first-class mail to: Harlequin Walk Down the Aisle Contest 1197, (in the U.S.) P.O. Box 9076, 3010 Walden Avenue, Buffalo, NY 14269-9076, (in Canada) P.O. Box 637, Fort Erie, Ontario L2A 5X3, Canada.

   Limit one entry per person, household address and e-mail address. Online and/or mailed entries received from persons residing in geographic areas in which Internet entry is not permissible will be disqualified.

3. Contests will be judged by a panel of members of the Harlequin editorial, marketing and public relations staff based on the following criteria:

   - Originality and Creativity—50%
   - Emotionally Compelling—25%
   - Sincerity—25%

   In the event of a tie, duplicate prizes will be awarded. Decisions of the judges are final.

4. All entries become the property of Torstar Corp. and will not be returned. No responsibility is assumed for lost, late, illegible, incomplete, inaccurate, nondelivered or misdirected mail or misdirected e-mail, for technical, hardware or software failures of any kind, lost or unavailable network connections, or failed, incomplete, garbled or delayed computer transmission or any human error which may occur in the receipt or processing of the entries in this Contest.

5. Contest open only to residents of the U.S. (except Puerto Rico) and Canada, who are 18 years of age or older, and is void wherever prohibited by law; all applicable laws and regulations apply. Any litigation within the Province of Quebec respecting the conduct or organization of a publicity contest may be submitted to the Régie des alcools, des courses et des jeux for a ruling. Any litigation respecting the awarding of a prize may be submitted to the Régie des alcools, des courses et des jeux only for the purpose of helping the parties reach a settlement. Employees and immediate family members of Torstar Corp. and D. L. Blair, Inc., their affiliates, subsidiaries and all other agencies, entities and persons connected with the use, marketing or conduct of this Contest are not eligible to enter. Taxes on prizes are the sole responsibility of winners. Acceptance of any prize offered constitutes permission to use winner's name, photograph or other likeness for the purposes of advertising, trade and promotion on behalf of Torstar Corp., its affiliates and subsidiaries without further compensation to the winner, unless prohibited by law.

6. Winners will be determined no later than November 15, 2001, and will be notified by mail. Winners will be required to sign and return an Affidavit of Eligibility form within 15 days after winner notification. Noncompliance within that time period may result in disqualification and an alternative winner may be selected. Winner of trip must execute a Release of Liability prior to ticketing and must possess required travel documents (e.g. passport, photo ID) where applicable. Trip must be completed by November 2002. No substitution of prize permitted by winner. Torstar Corp. and D. L. Blair, Inc., their parents, affiliates, and subsidiaries are not responsible for errors in printing or electronic presentation of Contest, entries and/or game pieces. In the event of printing or other errors which may result in unintended prize values or duplication of prizes, all affected game pieces or entries shall be null and void. If for any reason the Internet portion of the Contest is not capable of running as planned, including infection by computer virus, bugs, tampering, unauthorized intervention, fraud, technical failures, or any other causes beyond the control of Torstar Corp. which corrupt or affect the administration, secrecy, fairness, integrity or proper conduct of the Contest, Torstar Corp. reserves the right, at its sole discretion, to disqualify any individual who tampers with the entry process and to cancel, terminate, modify or suspend the Contest or the Internet portion thereof. In the event of a dispute regarding an online entry, the entry will be deemed submitted by the authorized holder of the e-mail account submitted at the time of entry. Authorized account holder is defined as the natural person who is assigned to an e-mail address by an Internet access provider, online service provider or other organization that is responsible for arranging e-mail address for the domain associated with the submitted e-mail address. **Purchase or acceptance of a product offer does not improve your chances of winning.**

7. Prizes: (1) Grand Prize—A Harlequin wedding dress (approximate retail value: $3,500) and a 5-night/6-day honeymoon trip to Maui, HI, including round-trip air transportation provided by Maui Visitors Bureau from Los Angeles International Airport (winner is responsible for transportation to and from Los Angeles International Airport) and a Harlequin Romance Package, including hotel accomodations (double occupancy) at the Hyatt Regency Maui Resort and Spa, dinner for (2) two at Swan Court, a sunset sail on Kiele V and a spa treatment for the winner (approximate retail value: $4,000); (5) Five runner-up prizes of a $1000 gift certificate to selected retail outlets to be determined by Sponsor (retail value $1000 ea.). Prizes consist of only those items listed as part of the prize. Limit one prize per person. All prizes are valued in U.S. currency.

8. For a list of winners (available after December 17, 2001) send a self-addressed, stamped envelope to: Harlequin Walk Down the Aisle Contest 1197 Winners, P.O. Box 4200 Blair, NE 68009-4200 or you may access the www.eHarlequin.com Web site through January 15, 2002.

Contest sponsored by Torstar Corp., P.O. Box 9042, Buffalo, NY 14269-9042, U.S.A.

PHWDACONT2

If you enjoyed what you just read,
then we've got an offer you can't resist!

Take 2 bestselling love stories FREE!
Plus get a FREE surprise gift!

Clip this page and mail it to Harlequin Reader Service®

IN U.S.A.	IN CANADA
3010 Walden Ave.	P.O. Box 609
P.O. Box 1867	Fort Erie, Ontario
Buffalo, N.Y. 14240-1867	L2A 5X3

YES! Please send me 2 free Harlequin American Romance® novels and my free surprise gift. After receiving them, if I don't wish to receive anymore, I can return the shipping statement marked cancel. If I don't cancel, I will receive 4 brand-new novels every month, before they're available in stores! In the U.S.A., bill me at the bargain price of $3.80 plus 25¢ shipping & handling per book and applicable sales tax, if any*. In Canada, bill me at the bargain price of $4.21 plus 25¢ shipping & handling per book and applicable taxes**. That's the complete price and a savings of at least 10% off the cover prices—what a great deal! I understand that accepting the 2 free books and gift places me under no obligation ever to buy any books. I can always return a shipment and cancel at any time. Even if I never buy another book from Harlequin, the 2 free books and gift are mine to keep forever.

154 HEN DC7W
354 HEN DC7X

Name	(PLEASE PRINT)
Address	Apt.#
City	State/Prov. Zip/Postal Code

* Terms and prices subject to change without notice. Sales tax applicable in N.Y.
** Canadian residents will be charged applicable provincial taxes and GST.
   All orders subject to approval. Offer limited to one per household and not valid to current Harlequin American Romance® subscribers.
   ® are registered trademarks of Harlequin Enterprises Limited.

AMER01   ©2001 Harlequin Enterprises Limited

...st from

HARLEQUIN

AMERICAN *Romance*®

and

Judy Christenberry

RANDALL PRIDE

HAR #885

She was the ultimate forbidden fruit. Surely now that lovely Elizabeth was engaged to another man, it was finally safe for Toby Randall to return home. But once he arrived, the rodeo star realized that his love for Elizabeth had only grown stronger and he'd let no man stand between them.

Don't miss this heartwarming addition
to the series

Brides

for Brothers

Available wherever Harlequin books are sold.

HARLEQUIN®

Makes any time special ®

Visit us at www.eHarlequin.com

HARRAND